# The other side

# of this side

## Johan Meiring

The Other side of this side

Published by Johan Meiring
Copyright © Johan Meiring 2018

Pietermaritzburg
Jameiring7@gmail.com

Originally published in Afrikaans as: " *Die KInd maar Mens"*
Copyright © Johan Meiring 2011

First Edition, first printing 2018
Edited by: Leigh Hunter
ISBN: 978-620-81031-9

Cover design by: Johan Meiring

Set in Malgun Gothic Semilight

In loving memory of

MAGDALENA ELIZABETH MEIRING

And

JOHANNES BARNARD MEIRING

# From the Author

Love is trust, trust at its purest. Love is being completely vulnerable and sharing this vulnerability with someone else. Love is falling into the unknown, letting go of fear and embracing the exhilaration. Love is about acceptance, forgetting expectations, passion, calmness sharing your life with someone and loving that person at your most honest, open, best, and worst times. Love is about always having faith in the other person and always having forgiveness and endurance in your heart. It is hard to love someone, and it is just as hard to lose someone. Life is all about the choices that we make. It is about the building blocks of life – pain, misfortune, abuse and resentment. Don't stop believing in yourself. Make peace with everything, learn to forgive and to move on. Suicide is never an option. It is all about forgiveness and to let go off our past.  Be free. Stop locking yourself up in the prison of your past. I hope you as the reader, enjoy this book, the story and the emotions that it may bring. Thank you for supporting this publication.

# Contents

Chapter 1.   Juan's Birth                                    1

Chapter 2.   Four Years Later                               16

Chapter 3.   A New Beginning                                27

Chapter 4.   Nine Long Months                               41

Chapter 5.   High School                                    61

Chapter 6.   Just Another Day                               90

Chapter 7.   Bloemfontein                                  100

Chapter 8.   A Year Later                                  116

Chapter 9.   Ronaldo                                       132

Chapter 10.  The Death of Juan's Mother                    146

Chapter 11.  Life Goes On                                  158

# Chapter 1.   Juan's Birth

Little Juan were born in the late afternoon of 18 June 1987 in a small rural town called Beaufort West. Elizabeth knew then she had been given the most precious gift that anyone could have ever received. A blonde little bundle of joy was lying in the incubator, Juan, with his whole family gathered around him. Elizabeth's first instinct had been to grab Juan up into her arms, to hold him so close to her, and kiss him over and over. Never has she dreamt of a beautiful moment like this. After a long tiring wait, the sound of cries that signalled the start of a new life brought tears of joy. As she holds her son against her chest, she cried tears of joy. Today they have met for the first time, but Elizabeth can't imagine her life without Juan. After a few minutes of hugs and kisses, Elizabeth lay him down in the incubator, folding the blankets over his tiny little body.

Juan's half-sister, Esmeralda, stood there gazing at him, smiling happily, eager to hold her little brother, she sneaked her finger through the opening in the glass to touch his tiny hand. Noticing how he held onto her finger, she said with glee, "Look, mother, he knows it's me! See how he holds my finger!"

"He knows who you are, Esmeralda, I'm sure he will be so proud to have a sister like you."

The doctor smiled at Juan's parents, wishing them well by saying, "God had given you a wonderful gift." Elizabeth decided then to call her boy Juan, although to her he would always be 'her little Juan'. The sun was setting when a nurse came to fetch Juan, being apart from him for the first time, Elizabeth replayed the happy first moments with Juan in her head over and over and continued for the rest of her life. Over the past two winter days, Elizabeth could hardly wait to see her little Juan, he stayed in the incubator in neonatal intensive care unit, NICU. Every now and then, she opened the drawers of the steel cabinet to have a look at the beautiful baby things in a wide variety of colours. She had brought far too many clothes for Juan, so there was more than enough to choose from when dressing up her son.

Elizabeth unwrapped some of the clothes, spreading them out on the hospital bed and trying to picture her boy dressed up in each outfit. The bright blue baby pants and green baby shirts were her favourites. Little shoes and socks, soft blankets, all these new things including her little Juan were a new beginning for Elizabeth. She was delighted when, at last, the moment came when they brought Juan back to her from NICU. Elizabeth asked the nurse to let Juan stay with her for a while longer than usual and the nurse on duty willingly gave her permission. Elizabeth could then quickly try some of the clothes on Juan. She tried on one after the other. This was the happiest days of her life.

"He is looking so sweet!" she told herself. Little Juan had become the world to her.

Elizabeth's mind was so filled with thoughts of Juan that she barely noticed the beautiful flowers and cards on the night-stand right next to her bed. The bouquet of flowers was filled with African violets, bunches of red roses with gypsophila and chrysanthemums. Juan was the only thing on her mind, nothing else matters to her at that time. After a few minutes of Elizabeth talking to her bundle of joy, in a language she taught he could understand, he fell asleep quietly and blissfully in her soft arms. For a while, Elizabeth listened to him breathing, thankful to know, undoubtedly, that his healthy little heart was beating inside his body.

Many visitors who came to see Juan that afternoon left the hospital with big smiles and much love for the new born boy, but nothing compared to the feeling Elizabeth had in her heart, one of absolute love – something she had not felt in many years. While the visitors were busy talking to Juan, Elizabeth picked up the Bible and opened it at 1 Corinthians 13: 4–8, which read: 'Love is patient, love is kind, it does not envy. Love is not jealous or boastful; it is not arrogant or rude. Love does not insist on its own ways. It is not irritable or resentful. Love does not rejoice over wrongdoing but rejoices at the truth. Love bears all things, believes all things, hopes all things and endures all things. Love never ends.'

As she read those words, that would remain with her forever, she heard the head nurse calling the door, "I'll be coming to fetch him in five minutes." Elizabeth quickly put the Bible down and heard a lady saying: "Isn't he just a lovely baby!"

"Thank you so much, I agree. Do you have any children?"

"I did have a child once, but God decided to take her to a better place."

"Oh, I am so awfully sorry to hear that." Elizabeth said with sorrow in her voice.

"Please, don't worry, I've had enough time to come to terms with my loss and to make peace with the situation."

"I am glad to hear you are in a good space, considering. I suppose you still have a clear memory of her birth?"

"Yes, quiet! It was difficult, to say the least – very painful indeed, but despite all the pain I gave birth to my beautiful Benita."

Elizabeth wanted to ask her about what had happened, and how her child had died, but she could feel the tears building in her eyes, she simply gave the lady a smile and a hug.

"I remember just saying over and over," the lady said a trembling voice "I want her back. I would have given anything to go back to the hospital and hold her again or to kiss her soft little cheeks."

The lady began to cry, which made Elizabeth cry as well, with tears poured down their sorrowful faces. The lady was young, around her mid-twenties, still so innocent. Elizabeth thought that to lose a child, no matter the mother's age, is devastating, the pain must be unbearable.

The lady told her that after the passing of her baby, she had put the clothes that her baby was wearing in a sealed bag to keep the smell. At times when the loss became too much to bear, she would open the sealed bag, just to get the smell of her baby again, then sealed the bag straight away just to keep the smell alive.

The story Elizabeth heard that day about a mother's love gave her the courage to love someone and not be loved in return. She was so grateful for her gift, she gave Juan one last kiss as the head nurse came to fetch him. The moment the nurse took him from her arms she was too scared to let go of him, as if he was a part of her.

"You really should rest now," the nurse said to Elizabeth, taking Juan in her arms. "I will be back in a while to check that you have eaten your food."

"Thank you, sister, thank you so much for everything."

"It's a pleasure!" the head nurse cheerfully replied.

After she had left with Juan, Elizabeth struggled towards the wash-basin and turned on the tap, filling it up with warm water. Stirring the water with both hands, she thought about the wonderful sensation of the hot water on my skin. She used the rough white towel hanging next to the wash-basin to dry her face and felt refreshed. Slowly Elizabeth returned to bed after which she fell asleep.

Elizabeth woke up much later that afternoon and went to the bathroom, on her way back from the bathroom she noticed Juan's father coming towards her in the passage.

"What a wonderful surprise!" she said. "So, you decided to come early!"

"Yes, I could barely wait to come and say 'hello'" he smiled.

The impression she got was that, although he already had children from his previous marriage, he had never seemed to be so happy as he was just then. Elizabeth realised that none of his children had ever tried to contact him, not even at Christmas nor on his birthday. What was he feeling and what passed through his mind as he gazed at Juan, Elizabeth would never know.  They both were so blessed, not only with a child but a whole new life that lay ahead for them. That day in the hospital signalled the beginning of our new life.

A nurse came into the room saying, "It's not visiting hours yet, so please don't take too long!"

"Don't worry, sister, we won't!" Elizabeth replied while she was admiring every centimetre of Juan and stroking his head.

Only too soon was the nurse back to fetch Juan. She left the room with a smile on her face talking to Juan and his father decided to leave a few moments later. "I have to go now. Take care and let me know if there's anything you need!" he said, kissing Elizabeth on the cheek.

"I will, and thanks for coming."

"It's a pleasure, my dear, this was just so unforgettable!" he replied.

Elizabeth watched as he left through the door, she turned on her side and closed her eyes.

Elizabeth had a dream she was lying on her back upon a cold, marble floor along with thousands of other people. Suddenly the marble floor broke in two and she woke up under water, the water was warm and crystal clear, she found out she could breathe underwater. Without any worries, no hunger, nor pain, without any effort, she was flying through the water. At this point she was flying with no person around but dancing with dolphins. She could even see stars on the bottom of the ocean. Suddenly she was jolted back to reality, woke up and laid in bed for a while, staring at the ceiling.

In the passage there was a noise that never seemed to stop. Somehow, amid all the distant crying, and hurrying footsteps, she thought she heard someone whispering.

In a dream sate, Elizabeth fell asleep again but was shortly woken up to the sound from the passage. There was a guy looking like a hobo, staring straight at her. At first, she just stared back at him frozen in fear, but then reached for the button – the one in red – to call for help.

The nurse on duty came rushing in. "What's wrong?" she asked.

"I saw a hobo staring at me through the door, from the passage!"

She went to the door to look around, but there was no hobo in sight. She just shook her head, continuing with what she was busy with. Elizabeth went to have a look myself to put her mind at ease.

"I could swear I saw someone in the passage. He woke me up. I saw him sitting on the floor, leaning his back against the wall." Elizabeth replied with the look of confusion on my face.

"I will ask security to come and have a look around," the nurse promised. "Just calm down and get back into bed."

"Am I losing mind?" Elizabeth thought to herself, in a daze as she sat up on the bed with white linen. "Could it be then that I was so afraid of losing my baby that I had seen a danger that did not even exist?" For a while, she sat staring out the window at the flowers and people outside, still thinking she could swear she saw someone or maybe she was just tired. Restlessly, Elizabeth made herself comfortable, laying back down in bed, closing her eyes, breathing slowly, thinking about her new-born baby, her new life and how things could change for the better. With those positive thoughts, she fell asleep.

Early the next morning, when the doctor made his rounds, he agreed that Elizabeth could go home in the late afternoon. She was so thrilled and could hardly wait to show Juan his new room – his own little nest, filled with baby paraphernalia, clothes, and toys. Not that he would understand what was going on, but Elizabeth just pretended he did.

Juan's father managed to arrange a lift to fetch Juan and Elizabeth from the hospital. The other passengers in the car were charmed, and even envious, when they saw Juan in Elizabeth's arms. They too, thought he was the most beautiful baby in the world.

Elizabeth had barely settled at home when friends and family started coming to visit her little Juan. It was as though there was a non-stop party going on with all the people wanting to say 'hello', to touch or to pick him up. All the baby-talk astonished Elizabeth as the visitors tried to communicate with Juan, sounding rather like a large litter of puppies competing for his attention, while he was quite happy to please them. This just made Elizabeth see how truly blessed she was. So many others craved for just such a little bundle of joy yet only some are fortunate enough to be granted that privilege, and now she was among those lucky ones.

That night Elizabeth fell asleep with her little Juan lying between her and his father. For the first time in a long while, there was a reason for them to go to sleep next to one another. Juan was the link that bound them together in a chain of love. Through him, they started to live and to become rich with love. From then on, each new day was a blessing, how quickly they seemed to pass. For weeks they were one of the happiest families in the neighbourhood.

Early that morning the sun smiled through the opening in the curtain with a mellowness and it was almost as if Elizabeth could smell something soft and fragrant in the light. Juan climbed over her and his father and woke them with his baby talk, only to fall asleep again on his father's chest. For a while, they slept again - until Juan started pulling the hair on his father's chest to let him know that he was now fully awake.

Luckily, Juan was not the kind of baby that would keep his parents awake at night by running around the house, a good night's rest was one of the gifts he gave his parents. This became their new daily routine. For years they would wake up with a smile, watching him grow, sharing his laughter, joy and memorable endless naughty behaviour.

--------------

If one day, you wake up tired, feeling down and sad, in a tight place so to speak, a place where you are not totally where you wanted to be, but still closer than you were before, even though it feels so distant and that you don't have the motivation in life that you need, or what you used to have, just smile and surround yourself with positive people, forget all the insults, trust your mind.

There will always come a time in our lives when we will feel tired, when we will be sad, the times when we will feel unappreciated and down. Always remember that there is no problem, no obstacle too big for you to handle. Just believe in yourself. Let your endurance grow and before you know it everything will fall in place. Do not be afraid of what life may throw at you, take it on with both hands and turn those negative things into positive things.

Don't get discouraged, these things that life throws at us, only makes us stronger. Stop trying to move the mountain. At the end the mountain is moving us, changing us in a good way so that we can be better prepared for life's battles. Our problems and troubles that we face are all momentarily.

The gifts life gives us outweighs all negativity. See troubles, problems, pain, and failures as lessons. We need these troubles and emotions in life to make us strong. In life it is okay to be tired, it is okay to lose something or someone. It is okay for you to feel pain and suffering.

# Chapter 2.   Four Years Later

Elizabeth was sitting on the floor, looking up at the photos on the refrigerator door and remembering the time when Juan had been so sweet and innocent – just a little infant sleeping in her arms. Since then, he had been growing bigger and stronger every day, learning new things and amazed his parents with his progress.

The dog was sleeping in a patch of sunlight in front of the window, the clean laundry had been hung out on the line to dry, while the food was cooking on the stove. This was just another ordinary day in their lives, except for one thing - little Juan was not at home as always.

Monday had been his first day at school. Elizabeth could see Juan in her mind, confidently walking through the school gate, not even once looking back. He was so fully taken up by the prospect of going to school, making new friends and playing with new toys. When his father had gone to pick him up after his first day at school, he was too proud to let his father kiss him in front of the other kids.

Elizabeth glanced up at the wall clock. Seeing that it was half-past one already, she switched off the stove and started to prepare lunch. Shortly afterward her little Juan and his father walked in.

"Mommy, Mommy! Look what I made you today!"

Juan pushed a drawing under her nose and she took it from him to have a look. It was a face with big red lips, pink cheeks, and long brown hair.

"My goodness, did you really do this?"

"Yes, yes, yes! Look there, at the bottom, our teacher also wrote my name on it!" '15 January 1991' was written in big red letters under 'Juan'.

"Oh, this is so beautiful! Is it a picture of me?"

"Yes!" Juan replied quickly.

"Thanks, my silly monkey, Mommy will keep this in a safe place."

She went to put it on the album that she kept in the small cupboard in the bedroom. When she returned to the kitchen, she found Juan had already gone outside to play, not even once thinking about lunch. Through the kitchen window, she could see him playing under the big fig tree in the backyard, while his dog, Vlekkie, was running in circles around him, trying to get Juan's attention. The two of them were sworn friends and understood each other perfectly. She was the gift Juan's parents gave him when he turned four.

Later, grubby from playing in the mud and soil all afternoon, Juan walked into the kitchen with a sad look on his face.

"What's the matter?" Elizabeth asked. "Why are you sulking?"

What followed was a tongue-in-the-cheek story about Vlekkie trying to persuade Juan to go fetch her something to eat, as well as many other sly little tricks that Vlekkie had been playing on him. His parents couldn't stop laughing at all the funny stories Juan had made up. Elizabeth warmed up Juan's plate of food, in the meantime, Vlekkie also got her plate of food. There were a few minutes of silence in the kitchen as Juan and his best friend ate happily. For the rest of the afternoon, Vlekkie was keeping Juan busy, the two of you were inseparable.

The sun was already setting behind some low dark clouds when Elizabeth told Juan that playtime is over.

"Time for your bath, my angel!" She called out.

Juan went to his room sulking, and not surprisingly, he soon started crying. Elizabeth thought 'How difficult it is for a child to have his play time interrupted, but if you could play with your toys and the dog, you were content.'

In the meantime, Albert, Juan's father, had finished running Juan's bath water and was already laying in bed watching TV. After a while Juan emerged from his room in the nude, carrying a car in each hand. "Mommy, is it okay if they come and bath with me?"

Elizabeth's patience had been wearing thin but realised that this could be the best way to get him into the bath without struggling, so in they went with him.

By half-past nine that evening, Esmerelda came to pick him up. Tonight, he will be spending the night with his sister. After they left, Elizabeth went straight to bed. It has been a very long day for her. For both his parents.

Late that night, Elizabeth was awakened by a noise coming from the kitchen. She got up, went to the door and looked down the passage to try and see what was going on. She walked to the kitchen and saw Albert sitting drunk at the kitchen table when suddenly, his fists came down on the table with a loud bang. She got such a fright that, for a moment, everything seemed to have come to a standstill. In a panic, she turned around in her place to creep back to the bedroom, but he had already caught sight of her and halted she in my footsteps when he shouted at her.

"Come here!" he shouted repeatedly.

Her heart was throbbing violently, she made her way into the kitchen and again he banged his fists on the table.

"What's this?" he asked her.

"The food I made earlier today," she replied with hesitation.

"Are you giving me this garbage to eat?" he replied with a dull smile on his face.

Elizabeth was stunned and, for a moment, stood there just a gaze at him. Quickly she turned around and walked away, but he followed her, grabbed her shoulder and slapped her hard across the face. For a moment there was a heat and stinging sensation on her cheek before she became aware of the searing pain.

Elizabeth fled outside through the back door and sat down on the bench in the yard, fearing that he might come after her. For a few hours, she just sat there in a kind of stupor, nervously on the alert for any movement or sound that might indicate his coming from the kitchen.

She walked back slowly and very cautiously opened the door, he wasn't in the kitchen. 'Thank God' she thought, 'he must have fallen asleep.' Quietly she sneaked into the bathroom, locked the door and faced herself in the mirror. Purply-blue bruises had appeared like streaks of paint smeared across her face.

Using a small sponge and some make-up, she carefully covered her cheek and lower eyelid in front of the mirror in the bathroom. A tear welled up in the corner of her eye, and she had to stop it from running down by using her fingertip. One side of her face was already slightly swollen up. Elizabeth heard footsteps stomping towards the bathroom. The feeling of being loved and protected had gone long gone away and the atmosphere was now tense.

Elizabeth decided to go sleep in one of the other rooms. She couldn't spend the night near him. She was too afraid and overwhelmed with anger and pain.

Early the next morning she heard somebody at the door. Her heart was throbbing in her throat.

"Mommy, Mommy!" Juan called out, and she knew then Esmeralda had brought him home. Relieved, yet anxiously, Elizabeth quickly went to the kitchen door, motioning to the two of them to be quiet.

"Shush! Your father is sleeping!"

Elizabeth hugged Juan tightly, but a tear betrayed the painfulness of her injuries and revealed the bruise on her face.

"Mom, what's going on? Why are there marks on your face?" Esmeralda asked.

"It's nothing, my darling, nothing at all," Elizabeth said as she felt yet another tear running over her cheek. Trying to brush those tell-tale tears away with her hand, the make-up she had applied so carefully was ruined, and the bruises were easy for anyone to see.

"Why is your face so swollen up?" Esmerelda asked.

"I slipped and fell in the kitchen on the wet floor as I was washing the floor."

"Has dad been hitting you?"

"I've told you already that I fell in the kitchen!" Elizabeth replied in a raised voice.

There was a heaviness in Elizabeth's hands as she slowly made her way to the kitchen to prepare breakfast. She felt the tears coming back into her eyes as she went about her task, but carefully wiped them away when she heard the bedroom door creaking. How unbearable and dreadful the morning became for her. Elizabeth tried to carry on, as usual, putting the food on the stove and hanging the washing out on the line. Albert sat down directly in front of the window and seemed to be staring at something out there, not once looking in her direction, neither could she look him in the eye. For the rest of that afternoon, Elizabeth spent lying in bed watching TV, while Albert sat in his chair in the kitchen until later that evening.

This was like that first time in the hospital when Elizabeth realised that a new phase in her life had begun.

-----------------

With alcohol abuse, you push the world aside, and you literally push your life aside, your friends and family for alcohol. Alcohol becomes the centrepiece in your life. Before you know it, it will take control of your life.

One thing that all of us should remember is that alcohol is not our friend. It is a toxic relationship. The same as an abusive relationship or marriage. Alcohol will take anything and everything from you until you have nothing left. Any addiction makes life, even more, harder than it already is, and not as easier as you have expected.

Many of us don't drink because we had a crummy childhood or suffered from a personal trauma. We drink because we are physically addicted to alcohol. Once they started drinking, they simply can't stop until they are flat on the floor, drowning in vomit and complaining of headaches and nausea the next morning. Alcoholism is not just an addiction, it is a disease. One that is manageable.

Like many other, people get drunk to drink away their problems or to forget about their problems, but when the morning comes, everything is still the same. Nothing changed. The problems are still there. Alcohol will only cause more problems and more pain in the long run.

# Chapter 3.   A New Beginning

The wind was sighing in the trees as Elizabeth switched on the kettle and arranged the mugs to make her family some coffee.

There was a sombre atmosphere around the house and she could see that her little Juan was keenly aware of this. While she escaped to the bathroom to try and hide her distress, Esmeralda finished making the coffee.

Sitting at the kitchen table, her family drank their coffee in silence. As Juan sat leaning against her, she held him close to her, knowing how Juan loved her with all his heart. After the discussion between Albert and Elizabeth that morning, there was now a brooding silence in the home. Clearly, the reason for his unwillingness to talk was her bruised face, he knew all too well his conduct was in the spotlight, and although he was guilty, he felt no remorse.

"What are we making for dinner tonight?" Esmeralda asked.

"I haven't quite made up my mind yet. Perhaps meat with potatoes, green beans, and rice."

"Sounds yummy, Mom! Could we have beetroot as well?" Juan asked.

"Yes, of course! Esmeralda, go and see in the steel cupboard if there is any left, please?"

Albert still sat there gazing through the kitchen window without looking at any of his family. He took a gulp of coffee every now and then, maintaining a stubborn silence.

The clouds had gathered in the sky, Elizabeth and her kids were busy peeling potatoes. She felt the roughness of the potatoes in her hands. "Is this what life was meant to be? Just dry, scratchy and dull like potato peels?" she wondered aloud.

"What do you mean? Do you really hate peeling potatoes so much?" Esmerelda questioned her mother.

"No, I don't mind peeling potatoes, what I mean is...must life be as hard and dry and scratchy as these peels are?"

"Mom, you know well enough that is not how it should be. We are all here for a reason. One reason is to be happy, another is to help other people in some way."

"Yeah, once upon a time I was happy, but now I am just plain miserable."

"It will pass Mom and all these bad feelings will be something of the past."

"Well, I hope this is the last time. Even though it happened for the first time, it feels as if it has been going on for years."

"Try not to think of it, Mom. You will soon be feeling better about everything!" Esmerelda comforted her mother.

"I really do hope you're right. Let's hurry with these potatoes, otherwise, there won't be any food on the table tonight!"

Elizabeth and her kids went on working in silence. She was surprised to hear Albert calling to her softly. As their eyes met one another's, she went into the bedroom and sat down on the bed.

"I'm terribly sorry! I didn't mean to hurt you," he said quietly.

"Very well, Albert!" she replied, getting up and starting to walk away.

"Ellie! I wasn't myself! I promise this will never happen again!" he called out to her, almost as if he cared.

"I forgive you Albert just pull yourself together, food is almost ready," she replied, trying to stay strong.

Afterward, Elizabeth sat down on the edge of the bath and looked at herself in the mirror, closely inspecting the marks on her face.

The wounds no longer hurt, but there was an aching pain, a feeling of betrayal deep inside of her. A feeling that she would never be able to forget. Elizabeth's family had always been so happy and even though they didn't have any earthly riches, they had one another and were blessed to have what they had, or so Elizabeth thought. 'Why was this happening to us? Was it all just part of marriage? Is this what it meant to stick together through thick and thin?'

Elizabeth washed her face, pulled herself together, and made her way through to the kitchen. "Come and wash your hands. Food is on the table and be quick!" she said to her kids.

Her family all sat down to eat, while Esmeralda carried the dishes to the table so that everyone could help themselves to meat and chicken, roast potatoes, green beans, carrots, sweetened pumpkin, and beetroot. The beetroot was one of the things which they usually only had on Sundays. Today Elizabeth made it special just for her little Juan, he always just loved beetroot.

Through the clattering of knives and forks there suddenly came the sound of knocking on the door. Esmeralda got up and went to have a look through the peephole before opening the door.

"Mom, you won't believe this! Just guess who's here."

Everybody looked up and saw Jannie, Juan's half-brother, walking into the kitchen.

"My goodness, Jannie! Where do you come from?"

"I was in the neighbourhood, so I thought I'd stop by."

"Sit down, my child. Are you hungry? Would you like something to eat?"

"I'm starving! It looks as if I'm striking it lucky! That would be great, Mom!"

Elizabeth and her kids were all gathered there around the table, by then a considerable change in the atmosphere of their home had taken over.

Early the next morning, as the sun lurks through the windows, Elizabeth saw that the grass was still wet after the light rain that had fallen during the night. After sitting up late with the rest of the family the night before, she did not even have the energy to close the curtains before going to bed. Everybody was still asleep, except her, the mother of the house, she had her daily routine to follow.

Elizabeth had been awake for some time already before going to the kitchen and filling the kettle with water from a plastic jug. She stood leaning with her back against the steel cabinet, listening to the kettle humming its little tune as it came to a boil. She remembered when she was still a young girl, her father used to put the kettle on the coal stove early every morning and how it used to make a loud whistling sound. At six o'clock having made his coffee, he would carry it out to drink on the veranda. Up until that day, she could still smell the fresh aroma of his coffee. Sighing deeply, she made herself a mug of coffee and spread some butter on a slice of white bread. 'How peaceful it was to sit down at the table to enjoy the coffee and bread!' she thought.

Juan walked into the kitchen, small wonderer - it was a Saturday morning. On the weekends Juan loved to be up and about early in the morning before the rest of the house. During the week, when he had to wake up for school, Elizabeth had a tough time getting him out of bed.

"Good morning, my son, have you slept well?"

"Yup!"

"Can I make you a sandwich?"

"Yes please, Mommy, but no peanut butter, please!" her little Juan replied.

"I'll you make you some toast with marmite then."

"Okay!" little Juan replied while fiddling with his fingers.

As soon as she had handed him his toast, he went out through the back door and sat down in the sun on the veranda at the back of the house.  Vlekkie was by his side, eyeing the toast. Once Vlekkie had managed to make eye contact with Juan, he understood she wanted, broke off a piece that Vlekkie swallowed in a single gulp, licking her lips for more.

The rest of the household was also up by then. Esmeralda was in the bathroom, Jannie in front of the TV, and Albert sitting in his chair in the kitchen where he normally sat day after day.

Elizabeth thought 'Quite soon the time would come for Juan to go to high school. How the time had flown! The year was already coming to an end.'

The day had begun like any other, Elizabeth had to get up early to do the dishes, make Juan sandwiches for school, iron his clothes and take Albert his coffee in bed. At half past seven, she got dressed to go to work.

On my way to work, it occurred to her that such a beautiful day should be spent lying on a beach, enjoying the sun's soft touch on her skin. The sunny weather was ideal for swimming.

Elizabeth had another block to go when my employer, Hendriena, called her on her cell phone.

"Hello, it's Ellie speaking!".

"Hello Ellie, it's Hendriena.  Are you on your way to work yet?"

"Yes, of course! Is there anything that you wanted me to do?" Elizabeth replied with a wondering eye.

"No, not at all! But I've left an envelope with your name on it at the reception counter. Read it as soon as you have the time to do so!"

"Thanks, I'll do that."

"It's a pleasure. Enjoy your day!"

"The same to you!"

In Elizabeth's eagerness, she fumbled with the key to the hair salon where she worked at.  Once she had managed to open the steel door, she hurried towards the counter. There was a small pink envelope, conspicuously placed where she could not have missed it, she tore it open and started to read:

'Hereby, I, Hendriena, owner of Hendriena's Hair Salon, give you, Elizabeth, one month's notice. Due to poor business, we are forced to reduce our staff...or even to close down the business....'

Elizabeth tore the letter up and flung it on the floor. 'How did she dare do this to me?  For the past few years I had been working conscientiously, and now she was giving me notice by writing me a letter! What sort of gratitude was this?' Elizabeth though, upset and angry, she immediately locked up the salon and went home.

Elizabeth was feeling so jittery that she went and bought herself something to drink to steady herself; liquor. Suddenly, she thought, things just seemed to be going wrong. 'First, there had been the trouble with Albert and now this! What had I done to deserve this?' She kept asking herself this question over and over.

When she walked into the house, she must have looked like a thunderstorm.

"And now? What's the matter?" Albert asked.

"That flipping woman, Hendriena, wrote me a flipping letter, placed it in a flipping pink envelope - so sweet, so pretty! - just to let me know she no longer needs me! She's given me the sack, and what is her excuse? She must reduce her staff due to poor business. Can you believe it?"

"My goodness, Ellie, this is so unfair! I know you are feeling very disappointed and hurt right now, but maybe it's not such a bad thing after all!"

"How on earth can you say this?"

"Well, I feel she has been misusing you: you got underpaid. Even when you had to work after hours, she paid you nothing extra. That is just my opinion, of course!"

"Yes, yes, you're probably right, but what will I do now without an income?"

"What have you got there in that shopping bag?" Albert asked.

"A bottle of brandy! I am sick and tired, and I just want to have a drink now!"

Neither of them felt the need to talk any further, they started to drink, never thinking about what might follow.

--------------

None of us deserves to go through abuse. Whether it is physical, emotional or psychological. The wounds take forever to heal. The pain knocks on our doors more often than we expect. Life can be tough, but it is still beautiful and worth living for.

Nobody has the right to treat you unkindly, to use you or to abuse you. To say no to abuse, you must know yourself and to know what you stand for and to know who you stand against. To know your values, and when to say no. What we will accept, and what we are against. We need to know ourselves.

All different kinds of abuse are just as devastating as the other. Abuse often affects our inner thoughts and feelings as well as exert control over your life. You may feel uncertain about almost everything and feel unsafe in your own home. Abuse does not only destroy relationships and friendships, it destroys the relationship you have with yourself.

Abuse can vary from physical beatings to yelling, imitating, ignorance and swearing. In most cases, abuse is all about gaining control or power over each other or a situation. Emotional abuse can chip away your self-esteem, self-worth. It makes us believe we are nothing and have nothing. Abuse can lead to long-lasting effects such as major depression, anxiety, withdrawal, Inability to trust and ultimately suicide.

# Chapter 4.   Nine Long Months

The sun was losing its hold on the day. Within a little while, it had started to disappear behind the mountain as though the night was eager to drown the light in its darkness. It was cold, and even the children who usually played outside until quite late had gone inside.

Esmeralda came barging through the front door and made herself at home at the kitchen table. This had always been the place where the family would gather or sit down to have a chat with one another.

"I've been wondering if I could bring the children tomorrow. Julie's parents won't be at home for the day."

"Yes, of course, you know my grandchildren are always welcome." Said Elizabeth.

"Can you cook lunch as well mom? I will see what I've got at home and bring it along tomorrow morning."

"Yes, Esmeralda, by all means!"

"Thanks, mom, the children are by themselves and I must be on my way now. Sleep well!"

"OK! Sleep well!" Elizabeth replied as she walked to the front door and watched as her daughter got into her car and drove off. Elizabeth locked the door behind herself and went into the kitchen.

On the bottom shelf in the white kitchen cupboard, there were two big pots that Elizabeth used for heating her bath water. Having filled both with water at the sink, she switched on the stove and as it usually took about an hour before the water was warm enough, she lay on her bed to watch a program on TV while she waited for the water to be heated.

Once the water was ready, it was an effort for Elizabeth to carry those heavy pots of hot water to the bath. Carefully she mixed the water and soap to a lather on her arms, enjoying the feeling on her skin. First the one, and then the other, she lowered both legs into the water. For a moment she remained quite still while relishing the comforting warmth of the water. Elizabeth then lay down flat on her back to allow the water to splash over her face and hair.

For a few moments, she could forget about the troubles that had been weighing her down. Elizabeth thought, 'Like they say, we all have our crosses to bear and our dresses to wear.' Sometimes the weight was a bit too much for her, she barely coped, that was the times she looked deep inside the bottle, believing she could drink away her problems, just to find out that they all would be coming back to her. Sometimes with one or two more than what she had bargained for.

After a long, relaxing bath, Elizabeth went straight to bed and slept like a baby.

Early the next morning, Elizabeth was standing with the folded washing in her arms in front of the window. The neighbours were in their yard, apparently busy making 'potjiekos', while the children were running around, playing games. She sometimes wondered about this family, and why their children were in the habit of not attending school.

As Elizabeth was walking down the passage, she heard a car outside in the street and saw that it was Esmeralda. Boisterously, the children came running in at the front gate. Soon the kitchen floor was littered with toys: books, pens, crayons, dolls, and whatever else they could think of to bring along.

Shortly after lunch, they were quietly playing in the bedroom, while Elizabeth was doing the ironing in the lounge, that was when she heard one of the children crying:

"Please, Lord Jesus, don't let my sister die so soon!"

Elizabeth hurried down the passage as fast as she could.

René, the elder of Esmeralda's two daughters, stood with both feet in the fish tank, while Juané sat on her shoulders. The glass had cut into René's feet.

"What have you done?" Elizabeth cried out.

"We just wanted to take something down from the shelf, Granny." They answered together.

"Why didn't you call me?"

"Dunno," they cried out.

Feeling quite dizzy, Elizabeth washed the blood from René's feet.

"Your mom will have a heart attack when she sees this!" she said, carefully removing each glass splinter from her granddaughter's feet and ankles. Seeing that the injuries were even more serious than she had suspected, Elizabeth phoned Esmeralda without further delay. Esmeralda came in a mad rush and off they went to see a doctor. After an hour they were back home, René having received five stitches to each foot.

Like, two little patients, the two sisters were lying next to one another on the bed beside their grandfather, René with thick bandages around each foot and Juané sipping a cool drink from a bottle. The three of them were watching TV.

Just after six Esmeralda came back, still fuming. After yet another scolding, she bundled the children into the car and took them home.

Once they had left, Albert suggested to Elizabeth she buy liquor again. The previous time they did this, no harm had come of it and she thought it might do them good to have a drink. Elizabeth went to buy some at the nearest bottle store on the corner of the main street, a block and a half or so away from where they stayed.

As soon as she got home, she poured a drink each. As the alcohol started to take effect, all sorts of rather weird stories came up. Insults and accusations were thrown at one another.

"Mommy, what's going on? Why are you fighting?" Juan asked looking confused.

"Oh, go to your room, what do you know about fighting anyway?" Albert replied to Juan.

"Please don't talk to him like that, Albert!" Elizabeth shouted at Albert

"Now you're protecting him again?"

"He's my child and has done nothing wrong. Why do you take your anger out on him?"

"The two of you are the same - equally useless and stupid!" he said in a raised voice.

"What have you ever done for us as a family? Ever since this child was born, you have been sitting where you are sitting now – on the same chair in the corner! Perhaps that is how your parents treated you, and now you are taking it out on our son! Does that seem fair to you?" Elizabeth said back to Albert

He got up from the chair, slapped and pushed her, causing her to fall with her head against the sink.

Slowly Elizabeth got up and started to walk in the direction of the bedroom furthest down the passage, but Albert came running up behind her, grabbed her by the hair and slapped her so hard that she stumbled into the bathroom and fell into the bathtub. Besmeared with her own blood, she again got up, ran to Juan's room and locked the door behind herself and Juan. Utterly shocked, trembling with fear, and crying, Juan clung to her.

The sounds of Juan sobbing were as clear as little bells moving in the wind. Terrified, Elizabeth held Juan close, singing in his ear, a lullaby. Hoping it would calm them both down. Even though every sound felt like it was right there with them in the room. Tired of being scared all the time, Elizabeth just lay her body down on Juan's bed. Clinging to her little Juan, she fell asleep beside him on his single bed.

Later that night Elizabeth woke up. As she walked down the passage, she saw Albert lying on the bed. As she stood there listening for a while, she could hear him muttering in his sleep, but it was impossible to make out what he was saying.

Having made certain that he was fast asleep, she told Juan to go and wait next door at the neighbour's house. Hurriedly, Elizabeth tossed most of her and Juan's clothing into some black garbage bags and tied the ends of each with a knot. She then called one of the neighbour's children to help her carry the bags. That night the two of them slept in the dark and bitterly cold in the graveyard a stone's throw away from their home, without blankets to keep them warm or anything to eat.

While Elizabeth was almost paralyzed with fear and felt her heart throbbing in her throat, it was hard to imagine what her little Juan must have been going through. His eyes were wide open and his whole body was shivering of the cold. Every sound, even the slightest rustling of leaves in the wind kept them awake that seemingly endless night. Never had she wished more fervently for the sun to rise, famished, and stiff from the cold, they fell asleep at long last.

The sound of a truck passing by soon woke Elizabeth up. The sun was now slowly but surely diving away from the night. With her eyes wide open, she sat quite still, contemplating their situation: this was the last time that she allowed her child and herself to be mistreated in any way. Now was the time to prevent it from going any further and from happening again.

It was already broad daylight when Elizabeth woke Juan up. She let him take shelter with the neighbour's house while she phoned her brother who was living in what was then known as the 'Transvaal'.

"Piet, I am sitting with a problem now. Will it be possible for me and little Juan to come and stay with you for a few days?"

"I don't think it should be a problem. When are you planning to come?" he questioned.

"To be quite honest, we are already on our way. I will explain everything as soon as I get there."

"So, when can we expect you here?"

"If we can catch the next train, we should be there by tomorrow afternoon."

"Okay, just give me a call from the station as soon as you've arrived, and we will come and fetch you."

"A thousand thanks, Piet! This means a lot to me and little Juan."

"It's a pleasure. See you tomorrow then!" confused, Piet said as he hung up.

Having put the receiver back, Elizabeth immediately went on her knees to thank God for opening this window for them. She firmly believed that this was the solution to their problems and that they had been delivered from all evil. She hastily went to fetch Juan from the neighbour's house, again asking one of the children to help her carry their belongings. And so, she walked to the station with Juan and the other child beside her.

They arrived at the station and bought two tickets to Benoni, her brother's hometown. When the train arrived later that afternoon, they took their places in a compartment like two mischievous children. Luckily it was just the two of them. Still, they didn't have anything to eat, but they tried to forget about the worsening hunger pains by drinking water and sleeping. Towards the evening they could hear the rain falling gently on the roof of the train.

Juan sat gazing out into the dark. Once or twice every few hours they saw the lights of the towns they were passing by, some having more lights than others. It had grown much colder and the rain came down harder. The soft click-clack of the iron wheels on the rails and the clattering sound of the switch rails lulled Juan asleep.

Early the next morning, somebody knocked at the door.

"Good morning, madam. I'm just doing some inspection. Can I see your tickets please?"

"Of course!" Elizabeth replied. She had to rummage in a plastic bag to find them.

"Got it! There you are!"

Juan watched as the ticket examiner clipped the tickets with a clipper, making an odd-looking little hole in each.

"Thank you! Enjoy your trip!" he said.

When he had left, they stood looking out through the window in the passage, directly opposite our compartment door. They had a view of the wide-open country, dotted with scrubby grey bushes. After a while, Elizabeth had to take Juan to the toilet. How terrified he was of that strange-looking hole.

"There's no need to be scared, darling. That hole is there for a very good reason. What must go out, must go out. It can't stay here on the train." she said it in a funny voice to calm his fears.

"But what if I fall through that little hole?" Juan asked worriedly.

"Well, there you've got the answer! It's just a small little hole and look how big you are. How will you ever fall through it?"

Juan was reassured then and without further ado, answered the call of nature, duly washing his hands afterward.

Back in the compartment, they sat down and quietly looked through the windows of the train as the bushes came flying by.

"Mommy, how far is it still to go?"

"Not far at all, we will be there in just a little while."

There was another knock at the door. This time a young lady stood there holding a tray in her hands. "Would you like some coffee?"

"My goodness, don't tell me this is for free?" asked Elizabeth.

"Yes, of course! With our compliments."

"That would be great, thank you!" gracefully grateful they accepted the coffee.

"Thank you so much!" Elizabeth replied.

"It's a pleasure. Enjoy your trip!"

Having closed the door, Elizabeth cradled her cup in both hands and savoured the wonderful aroma. Then slowly, taking small sips, she drank the coffee. 'Such a blessing it was!' she thought, 'Like in the old days, we could still get coffee for free on the train.'

'Why had things turned out as they had?' 'What had we done to deserve all of this?' Asking herself these questions, she later noticed that their journey was coming to an end and was only too thankful when at last they arrived at their destination. After the train had come to a standstill, Elizabeth and Juan got out and went to the nearest phone booth to call her brother. Piet and his wife arrived soon afterward in a white Ford, both giving them a welcoming smile.

"Hello! Thank you so much for coming to fetch us."

"Don't mention it. I can hardly wait to hear what you've got to tell us!" replied Piet.

"This is going to be a long story. I will tell you everything later."

"I do hope so!" Piet said with a little laugh.

They all got into the car, and off they went at a speed. They didn't have far to go, and after a few minutes stopped in front of two enormous white gates.

"We're home!" Piet replied.

"Thank God!" Elizabeth said. Knowing they haven't eaten in two days.

"You must be dead tired!"

"Well, we're not as tired as we are starved for something to eat!"

"Haven't you had anything to eat on the train?" Piet asked looking at his sister with sudden shock and concern.

"No, we had our last bite of food the day before yesterday!"

"How is that possible?"

"I will tell you in a little while," she answered.

After they had carried the bags into the room where they were to sleep, while Juan was sitting on the couch in the lounge, Piet and Elizabeth had an opportunity to talk privately.

"Albert has been beating me up more than once! I just couldn't take it anymore, and now have decided to leave. Juan and I even spent a night sleeping in the graveyard. The following morning – that was yesterday – I phoned you." Elizabeth told Piet.

"This man must be a scoundrel to be abusing a woman in this way!"

"Now you people know what's going on. I don't want Juan to suffer anymore - he has already gone through too much."

"I can understand that. Please make yourself at home! You are welcome to stay for as long as you like." Piet comforted Elizabeth.

"Thank you, dear brother, you have no idea how much this means to me. Thank you for being there, thank you for helping us!"

"Rest assured, I will always be there for my sister!" Piet replied with a smile on his face.

After Elizabeth's talk with Piet, her and Juan went to shower. They then sat down on the couch, each with a plate of food, while the whole family chatted together about the good old days. Juan had fallen asleep in the meantime and Elizabeth went to lay him down in the bedroom, just like she used to when he was four years old.

Kissing him on the forehead, she made sure that he was fast asleep, before going back to the lounge where the rest of Piet and his family sat up until late that night. For a change, she thoroughly enjoyed herself. She was glad she had someone to talk to, to open up and to speak her mind.

The next morning, Elizabeth got up early to help to make breakfast. They were a big family and to get ready for the day, they all had to start getting ready earlier to give everyone a chance to bath or shower. One of the children had to get ready for school, while two others had to go to work. Elizabeth's sister-in-law was alone in the house during the day.

Some days passed before Elizabeth decided to stay on with the family and to enrol Juan at one of the local schools. A new school, new friends, and a new job – suddenly everything had changed and for Juan this proved to be one of the most difficult adjustments he had ever made. It became a nightmare for him, and Elizabeth later realised that he persevered only for her sake.

Every afternoon after school, Juan came home crying. He just couldn't adapt to the new environment, and the children taunted and made fun of him. When winter came, he had to go to school wearing short pants and a shirt, without a jersey for warmth. Not being able to afford new school clothes, Elizabeth had to make use of the school's clothing bank for second-hand school clothes.

After this had gone on for many months and in the end realising that neither Elizabeth nor Juan could ever be happy there, she had to reconsider their situation. She longed to go back to her own home, yet felt no desire to see my husband again, whereas Juan desperately wished, not only to be back in his own home, but also to be reunited with his father. At that stage Juan fully understood what had happened and why it had been necessary for them to leave, although this did not, for a single moment, prevent him from loving his father and yearned to go home.

It took Elizabeth nine long, bitter months to make up her mind to go back to Albert. In the meantime, he had phoned many times, begging her to return. Just like the first time, he promised me over and over never to hurt them again. Although Elizabeth was filled with pain and sadness at what he had done to them, she was still afraid of going home, she agreed to return for the sake of her little Juan.

---------------

For us to forgive people, we need to understand them. When people do hurtful things towards you, just know that they did not necessarily do it to you, but they did it to themselves. You were only a victim of their weakness. Whenever we want mercy, we need to have forgiveness in our hearts. We all are guilty of something at some point in our lives. None of us are perfect, and all of us deserves to be forgiven. We must forgive to sustain love. With this, nobody said you should allow someone to hurt, abuse or neglect you, this only means that you should enforce forgiveness. In life, nothing just happens. Everything happens for a reason, whether it is good or bad.

Our lives have been carefully orchestrated. Going through pain, death, loss and misfortune and many other things which may not seem fair to us, is key to make sense of the madness in our life. Never feel sorry for yourself. All our pain is the foundation, the building blocks of our life.

# Chapter 5.   High School

The early morning of Juan's first day in grade eight at Central High School, the only secondary school in the area where his family lived, had turned out cold and rainy. Juan had prepared for school, feeling rather apprehensive of what lay ahead for him. As he came to the door to leave the house, he stopped and turned around. "Mom, seeing that I am now going to high school, I no longer want to be little Juan, but Juan."

"Okay, but you will always be my little boy and sometimes I might just forget to call you Juan." Elizabeth replied smiling.

"It's okay if you forget now and then, but please, not in front of my friends!"

"I'll try, but you really should be running now. You don't want to be late on your first day in high school, do you?"

"Nope! Have a nice day, Mom!"

"Behave yourself, and remember, I'm waiting to hear about everything when you come home this afternoon."

"Okay, bye now!"

"Bye!"

Juan went down the street, proudly carrying his school bag slung over his shoulder. Luckily, he wasn't the only one who walked to school along this route and soon met someone to walk with him.

He had barely arrived at school, when he heard that all pupils in grade eight were classified as 'butter-heads' and soon enough learned the meaning of this, they were seen as inexperienced blockheads, which in turn meant that every grade twelve student was in the privileged position to adopt a 'butter-head' as a child and that the child had to obey the grade twelve student, also called 'the parent', at all times.

The butter-heads had to face many kinds of challenges, as well as do the special favours that were required of them. While having to carry the parent's schoolbags, buying them snacks at the tuck-shop, the butter-heads were also humiliated in front of the rest of the school. For Juan this was a nightmare and, as a result, he soon started hating the thought of going to school.

On that first afternoon, he returned home very unhappy and told his mom about the butter-heads. At first, she laughed, but noticing how upset Juan was, she tried to cheer him up with whatever words of wisdom she could think of. "It is good for you! It teaches you to be independent, you learn obedience, and not to talk back or question each and everything."

"But Mom, it is so unfair to be carrying someone else's schoolbag all the time!"

"It teaches you to have respect, especially for your seniors."

"Now that doesn't make any sense to me at all. I hate it!"

"Very soon this will be all over. Try to see the funny side of it and enjoy it!"

After six months, Juan had pretty much become used to be a butter-head. Although most of his fears and frustrations were dispelled by then, he still hadn't made many friends and felt left out. Many mornings, Juan sat alone on the steps in front of the school, waiting for the bell to announce the new school day, while the other kids were gathered in groups on the lawn. He sat there, staring longingly at the groups, wondering what the problem could be and the reason why he couldn't be a part of them like all the others.

During classes, nobody ever spoke to him, except when they needed to borrow a pencil or an eraser. He felt lonely and rejected. Deep within himself, he suffered, pitying himself, but never showing it. Like his father, Juan was too proud, even saying 'I'm sorry' was almost like begging for cookies in an orphanage.

One afternoon after school, Juan met a friend who often walked with him on their way home. About halfway, they noticed that some bushes close to the river were on fire. Juan's friend had a cousin living in a house on the river bank and seeing that the house was now in danger of catching fire, they immediately ran towards it. The cousin was already trying to fight the fire close to the house and they helped him by carrying water, bucket by bucket, to where he was busy quenching the flames. After struggling for half an hour, they succeeded in putting out the fire.

The two men who lived there invited Kianu, Juan's friend, and Juan in for coffee. Both being homosexual, they were busy watching an erotic homosexual movie on their TV screen. Juan was slightly shocked but joined them. Realising that he enjoyed it, Juan soon became absorbed in it. That same afternoon, Kianu and Juan experimented with what they had seen and for Juan, this was one of the best things that had ever happened to him. He experienced an immediate sense of being acknowledged as a person.

Suddenly, Juan was happy and content, the emptiness within himself having been replaced with the attention he had craved for such a long time. As from that day, Juan slowly but surely began to change, seeking consolation and each time finding it with a man.

It was just so interesting that Juan had any kind of attraction or orientation at all because at that age he thought he didn't have any kind of orientation, never mind sexual orientation. Fearing discrimination and being made fun of most of, Kianu and Juan tried to hide it. Juan did not feel any difference in the treatment from the other kids, but they felt that he was different.

To walk and talk and to show emotion through his body became an obstacle for him. He had to change himself time and time again just to fit in. Not to be the topic of a conversation. Juan really tried to hide who he was from everybody.

His parents suspected the truth but refrained from asking him any questions. After school every day, Juan quickly finished his homework and would then leave the house as inconspicuously as possible, only to return much later in the afternoon. His manner and attitude towards his parents had undergone a change by then, and he also felt more mature than others in the same age group as him.

The reason for this might have been his relationship with friends who were older than he was at that stage. Juan had many friends, which never knew about his sexual orientation, others who did know always asked him a lot of questions on an ongoing basis.

One afternoon, Juan met a teacher who wanted to give him a dog as a present. Unfortunately, his yard was not big enough to keep a dog and as a result, she afterward changed her mind. From then on, the teacher and him became friends. Juan used to visit her often, especially when the fighting and abuse continued between his mother and father. For him, it was his safe-haven. A place he can run to so that he can be freed of all the misery. He and his teacher would often walk the dogs every afternoon. During that time, he went along with her in her car on these outings. This was how he ultimately came to know so many kinds of birds. She went out of her way to teach him about the different species of birds in the grassland, where they occurred, what their habits were, and how each could be identified by its call. Within a short while, he had become quite an expert on the subject.

One afternoon Juan arrived home, eager to tell his parents about what he had learned, how many different species of birds he got to see. He was so excited, she also taught him how to drive for the very first time, only to find all the doors of the house locked, and the windows fastened. Juan was angry, yet also had an uneasy feeling about this.

He sat there for some minutes before his mother appeared at the gate. She was covered in blood, she had cuts on her arms and bruises on her legs and chest. When Juan saw how swollen up her eyes were, he immediately realised what had happened and started to cry. His mother tried to comfort him while explaining as well as she could, that his father had locked them out of the house. He was still inside the house and refused to open for them.

From within, Juan and Elizabeth heard his father repeatedly shouting that Juan wasn't his child and that they had to disappear from his life. He absolutely refused to allow them in to collect their clothes and his mother had to call in the police for assistance.

When the police arrived, they had to break the door open and upon entering the house, Albert came striding down the passage, ranting and chasing everybody away. When he saw that Elizabeth stood her ground, he again slapped her. The police then immediately took hold of him, dragging him down the garden path and having put handcuffs on him, flung him into the police van and drove off.

Juan was still outside, confused, devastated and broken. Everyone was looking at his family. The street was flooded with people. He didn't know what to do. Being devastated and scared Juan was overwhelmed with embarrassment all at the same time.

While Elizabeth put their clothes into bags, Juan made his way into the house, changed his clothes, and hurried to leave the house as soon as they could. Being confused and shaken at the same time, Juan forgot to pack his school uniform. That night Albert spent his first night in prison, while for Elizabeth and Juan it was the third time that they were to find themselves left out in the cold. Juan was crying out in desperation, asking himself 'Why this was happening to them.' He had believed his father when he promised never to let this sort of thing happen again. Elizabeth and Juan spent that night at Esmeralda's house, and the next morning Juan went to school barefoot and wearing ordinary clothes.

Although Elizabeth didn't want him to go to school, he had refused to stay, and as a result, everybody at school kept staring at him. In the register class, the teacher took it upon himself to make up a story explaining why Juan had come to school without his uniform.

Juan just couldn't handle the humiliation. It was the same old story over and over. 'How could my father live with what he had done to us, and why did he do it?' he thought. He couldn't go on fighting it anymore. He needed his father, not to be a father, but to be doing things together with him, to help him, and to be his friend, the kind of relationship with him Juan had never had. Instead, Juan lived in fear of his father and had now begun to reject him.

Juan's feelings towards his father started to change. He didn't want to see him again. The pain he caused made Juan feel like he hated him.

For many days Juan refused to see his father. On the contrary, Juan longed to see him, but at the same time, wished that he was dead. Instead of having fun and to be happy, living a normal childhood, life was passing Juan by. All he got was the pain, hurt, abuse and humiliation. His father took so many things away from him, from his mother, from their family.

It felt like only yesterday, Juan was sitting on the kitchen floor, being that four-year-old boy when everything was still perfect. His mother so happy, and his father too, whereas now he felt that they had become strangers to one another.  Just to show how quickly things can change.

Finally, Albert was released from the holding cell. It had been a few days, Elizabeth and Juan went back to their house. 'Why we always find ourselves back with him, is something I cannot explain,' thought Juan. Being pushed around from one home to another, different schools now and then, new friends every time, this is just a few things that made him want to hate his father for everything that he has done to him and his mother.

Early one morning, Juan's father started to complain about pain in his legs and was unable to stand up. He went to see the doctor and was told that his legs would have to be amputated.

After several weeks in the hospital, Albert was dismissed. Juan believed that his father had got what he deserved for all the pain and misery he put them through. Now he would no longer be able to chase his mother to beat her up.

Now that Albert was in a wheelchair, Elizabeth worked harder than ever to get the housework done. She had to bath him, switch TV channels, and generally had to leave off whatever she was busy with to do his bidding. She was already becoming physically weak and could no longer cope with all the work she had to do.

Even in his disabled condition, Albert did not stop humiliating Elizabeth. Her repeated asthma attacks had been a direct result of her abuse, and a few times she had to be taken up in the hospital to receive oxygen.

Three years had passed. Juan was now eighteen and in his final year of school. The history of violence in his parents' home and the memories of all that he had been put through made him eager to leave home as soon as possible. Juan could no longer live with the fighting that had become part and parcel of their lives weekend after weekend. The love between his parents had by now become a thing of the past.

Final year didn't turn out to be as bad as Juan had been made to believe by all those who got a kick out of unduly scaring him and the other students. In fact, Juan found that this could be the most rewarding of all one's school years.

One morning Juan was late for school, arriving when a class had already begun. Rather worried, he pushed the door open and entered, yet neither the teacher who was busy with the lesson nor my classmates who were attentively listening to her, seemed to be aware of his presence as he quickly went and seated himself at his desk. He found it very strange indeed not to be scolded by the teacher for being late, and for once, not to be stared at by the rest of the class.

By the time the second period started, Juan had caught up with the work and could continue in his usual unhurried manner. Only after the class had been dismissed, the teacher demanded an explanation.

"I'm sorry, miss, my school shirt, the only one I've got, was still wet this morning, and I had to get it dry and iron it myself."

"Although this explains it, it is still no excuse for being late. From now on you will see to it that you do the laundering the previous afternoon already. Is that understood?"

"Certainly, miss! I'm sorry, I won't let it happen again."

"You are excused and may go now."

Juan left the classroom, astonished. Later, during our second break, he was sitting in a circle with all his other classmates, both boys and girls. Light-heartedly, they were chatting about how the day had been going thus far, when Juan suddenly shocked them with some questions.

"Is it normal to care for a man so much, if you yourself are a man?"

"Gosh, I adore men. For me it is quite normal," Anna replied.

"But, Anna, this is because you're a girl. Of course, it is normal for you. But what about me, am I crazy?"

"No, you're not crazy. Everyone has his or her own idea of sexuality, and each of us knows what we feel comfortable with. I say, go for what you like, and what you know to be the best for you. Do whatever you are comfortable with!"

"Hmm...okay."

"And the most important thing is that you should enjoy it – just go for whatever makes you happy!" Anna replied.

"Definitely!" the others agreed.

"Gosh, guys, sometimes it feels wrong, and at other times I feel as if I couldn't be bothered who thinks or says what about me. All I know is that a man makes me happy."

"You go, boy!" Again, Anna replied.

The conversation trailed off, while Juan was gazing into the sky above and his thoughts ran their own course. He couldn't help reflecting on the life he had led thus far, for so long not having had companions on the school ground. Now, suddenly, it was almost unreal to have so many friends gathered around him.

Juan looked at them all, flashing them with a smile and showing him gratitude through a dull 'thank you' for being willing to be a part of his life.

The bell rang, and the break was over. The students all ran to the school building to be on time for the next class. Typing was Juan's favourite school subject. First, they would do a typing test before starting the new work. As usual, Juan was the first to have completed it and had to keep quiet while the rest of the class was still busy.

Once all the work had been handed in, everybody started chatting. Usually, the atmosphere in the typing class would be free and easy, with everybody exchanging wisecracks and having a seemingly unending supply of stories to share.

"Psst..."

Looking up, Juan saw Theresa trying to draw his attention.

"So, what seems to be the problem?" He asked.

"Guess who I saw yesterday?"

"Hmm...I have no idea, you'll have to tell me, or should I beg you?"

"Jovi!"

"Jovi? Where did you see him?"

"In the street!" she said hurriedly.

"In the street? That's no answer! In what street?"

"That I am unfortunately not able to tell you now. As long as you know that he is in town right now!"

"Hmm...thanks for the info, I will try to contact him later."

Our conversation was interrupted when the bell rang. The school day was over in the blink of an eye. Everybody was now in a rush to go home, and Juan too was making his way quickly across the green sports grounds, through the school gate, and across the river. Some short distance away from his home, Juan saw Jovi sitting on their front veranda.

Juan heart was beating fast, while everything else within him felt as if it had come to a standstill. As they hugged each other, Juan was overcome with joy, and quite speechless for a while. It had been almost nine months since they had last seen one another, although, on that occasion, things had turned out rather miserably for both. Even though they had parted quarrelling, Juan had the feeling that one day they would make up again.

"Hi! You came home quickly today!"

"Oh, not really!  I'm home this time every afternoon," Juan said, pausing for a moment before continuing, "Well, I heard that you are in town."

"I'm not surprised. The people here always have their noses in other people's affairs." Jovi replied laughing.

"Quite true! What brings you here so early today?"

"I was afraid of missing you and was thinking we might spend some time together this afternoon."

"Are you asking me, or are you telling me?" Juan asked.

"Both, actually!" Jovi replied.

"It shouldn't be a problem. Allow me some time to change quickly, have a quick bite and see if my parents will allow me to go." Juan replied being anxious.

"We can go and eat somewhere as soon as you're ready,"

"It's not really necessary. I will just..."

"This is on me. I want to do this for you – just say 'yes'!"

"Okay, I'll get ready then," Juan replied.

"Thanks, it's great seeing you again!" Jovi said with a smile.

"And it's great seeing you, too! Come on in and wait for me in the sitting room."

As Jovi seated himself quietly in the sitting room on one of the red leather couches, it felt like only yesterday that they had last seen one another. The unresolved feelings between the two of them wasn't making it any easier to look at one another as though there was nothing between them.

Juan noticed that Jovi got up to have a closer look at the photos in the display cabinet. To the left there was one of Juan when he had taken up modelling some years previously, posing on an old steam engine.

While Jovi was alone in the sitting room, waiting for Juan, he probably was thinking of their past relationship and assessing the strength of his feelings for Juan. Deep within himself, Juan knew he still wasn't ready for a relationship, and that probably the biggest constraint was him fearful of being hurt and having to start all over again to build up trust in the other person.

"I am ready to go now if you are!" Juan said.

"Yes, of course, I was just having a look at the pictures while I waited."

"They don't all quite come up to scratch - some are a bit boring, but ok, I suppose! "

Like bosom friends, they walked side by side down the street. On our way to town, they entered a shop to buy bottled water, before continuing their leisurely walk down the main street towards Saddles.

"Jovi..." Juan said.

"Uh?" he answered.

"Please don't be mad at me, but the feelings that I have for you are getting more and more intense, especially when you look at me like that!"

"No, I could never be mad at you. In fact, that is how I feel too! Believe me, those were precisely my thoughts while I waited for you in the sitting room."

"Gosh, am I glad to hear that! I thought you might have changed your mind about me in the meantime."

"No, man, of course not! I'm too mad about you to change my mind so easily."

There was a short silence then Juan, who had been waiting for this moment, thought 'Could this be the right thing to have said, even knowing that Jovi was the very reason why I felt so happy at that moment?' 'Jovi had stepped from a world of dreams, suddenly has become a reality.' 'The feeling was still somehow unreal, and I feared that it might all be just some short-lived delusion.'

"So, what planet are you on right now?" Jovi asked.

"Hmm...one not too far from here. I was thinking about us, and what would be the right thing to do." Juan replied.

"Perhaps we should just take it easy, stop thinking about what might go wrong, and give it a go." Jovi replied.

"Perhaps you're right, and we are just wasting our time now worrying about being perfect".

"I agree!" Jovi said quickly

"Yes, let's take the chance!" Juan replied confidently.

Having arrived at the restaurant, the waiter showed them to a table. Juan felt as if the love he had been waiting for had come. Yet, deep within himself, there was still a nagging doubt. 'I am young, how could I be certain of what still lay ahead of me that year?' He thought. 'Where was my life headed for anyway, and what would become of us if life took an unexpected turn away from whatever we might be planning?'

Juan had been through much pain already. It was easy to get hurt, and he was afraid of going through more suffering while he was still so young. Lost in thought, Juan was slightly startled when the waiter asked if they were ready to place an order.

"Orange juice for me, please." Jovi said, knowing exactly what he wanted.

"I'll have the same, thanks," Juan replied.

"Something to eat, perhaps?" the waitron asked.

"We'll just have the juice for now." Jovi replied.

"Good, I'll be back in a little while then."

"Thanks." Jovi replied.

"I'm willing to take a chance, but I'm not a hundred percent sure that's what I want to do," Juan told Jovi

"I understand, but if we don't try, we'll never know if it was meant to be." Jovi replied.

Soon the waitron returned, and they placed their order. The two continued their conversation in a laid-back mood. A waitron standing in the corner of the restaurant got wind of what was going on and immediately told one of his colleagues about the two. As always, there were people who found it strange to see two men in a relationship. Very few people have made peace with the idea that two men could have feelings for one another.

After the meal, they decided to return to Juan's house. Once there, they realised that they were all alone.

Together they went to Juan's room and opened their hearts to each other. Jovi suddenly started kissing Juan, and without any hesitation Juan was returning the kiss. While Juan kept his eyes closed and felt Jovi's warm lips on his own, he gently held the back of his head. Jovi went on kissing him as Juan slowly lay back on the bed, with Jovi on top of him. Whispering softly in his ear, Jovi asked Juan if he had ever experienced the stairway to heaven. Juan murmured that he had not and could not help laughing at the same time.

Juan then began to kiss Jovi more passionately, realising now that he wanted Jovi more than he wanted Jovi before. Detaching themselves from the world out there, Jovi kissed Juan on his cheek, and on his neck. As Jovi blew softly into Juan's ear, Juan lay powerless on the bed, sinking deeper and deeper into a world of his own.

Jovi took off his shirt and Juan followed suit. After another kiss, Juan moved upwards and kissed him lightly on his chest, moving slowly towards his navel. Juan moved upwards again, kissing him on his neck. Jovi lifted his head, and Juan could see that he was overpowered by an onrush of many different feelings all at once.

At that stage, they both wanted to go further but suddenly stopped. Neither of them was ready yet for such a far-reaching step, especially at that early stage of their relationship.

They decided to pull themselves together and went to sit outside in the garden instead. There were no feelings of guilt as they sat there chatting quietly in the calm of the evening. Later Jovi went home. After supper Juan went to his room, thinking about Jovi and what had happened between the two of them that afternoon. Still mulling over the situation, Juan must have fallen asleep, as he woke up later to a thunderstorm brewing in the distance.

The sound of the thunder drew closer, and it sounded as if someone was deliberately banging louder and louder on the roof, while lightning flashes were playing in the sky above the house. As the heavy rain poured down on the roofs and made a rattling sound of empty cooldrink cans, Juan got up from my bed and made himself a nice cup of coffee.

It was already half past one as he sat down in front of the window in his room. Peering into the pitch-darkness that was now and then interrupted by flashes of lightning, his childhood came back to him like a video being played back in his mind. With each clap of thunder, Juan expected something terrible to happen somewhere in the house between his mother and father. He wasn't sure if he heard their voices, but the slamming of a door cleared his wondering mind instantly. 'It must have been caused by a gust of wind,' thought Juan. He realised that he was overwrought, that the confusion of feelings of the day before, and the difficulties of his family life, had been wearing him down.

------------

Relationships are an ongoing change of interaction of knowledge through honesty and loyalty between two people. We need to make a conscious investment in each other build on trust and always remember to avoid assumptions. Throughout a relationship, we never stop to grow emotionally. We learn every day. Many of Juan's relationships failed, because it was all about him, and not about them. There were times when he would rather look at his phone first, before saying "good morning"

Never focus too much on yourself. Everything is not about you. We focus too much on what we are not getting, or what our partner is not giving us. We must be vulnerable enough, to be honest, and open always.

To take responsibility and ultimately to apologize for our actions. Even though we are all individuals, we need to be consistent in what we do. Relationships are based on communication, honesty, loyalty, trust, and intimacy.

The intimacy that can be differentiated between emotional, intellectual and experiential intimacy. All relationships need a form of intimacy to survive. We should not confuse intimacy with sex, even though sex is also a form of intimacy.

Intimacy is a process whereby we truly feel connected and known by our partners. Being emotionally intimate is extremely important. It allows us to be open and honest with each other. We can share and talk about our most inner thoughts, to share our joy and pain with each other.

Never thought I could feel like this again about someone, I had an overwhelming joy in my heart again.

# Chapter 6.   Just Another Day

Juan woke up the next morning and was on in the process of getting ready for school when he realised it was a Saturday. He got out of bed to inspect the calendar hanging behind his door. Indeed, it was a Saturday. He looked out through the window and saw the sun slowly rising over the top of the mountain, shining light into the rooms of the house. The grass was wet, carrying the fresh smell of the rain. Raindrops were suspended from the leaves of the small plants, each like a prisoner waiting to be released. All the plants had been washed clean by the rain and everything seemed renewed, even the streets and the roofs of the houses were sparkling in the morning sun.

Juan got back into bed, thinking, 'Not so many years ago, I would have heard my mother working in the kitchen, as she usually would, she would get up early every morning of the week. Her day would start with a cup of coffee before cleaning the kitchen and doing the laundry in the washing machine, and its screeching noise would wake up everyone in the house.' Juan was still in bed when he heard his mother in the backyard. Juan's father sat at the table in the kitchen, holding his mug of coffee and staring out the window.

Sitting alone in his room that morning, Juan reconsidered what had happened the previous day between Jovi and himself. They had known each other for quite a while already, and their feelings for one another were rather special.

More than once in the past, Jovi had tried to seek a closer relationship with Juan, and every time Juan had turned him down. Juan had been hurt too much in the past and was afraid of opening himself up again.

There were just too many issues to consider, not the least being Juan's troubled past; another was the fact that he was many years older than Juan. It had now become obvious to Juan that the conversation they had the previous day had only given both false hopes.

Even the intimate moments they had shared, now seemed meaningless. Soon Juan would finish his schooling career, and it was impossible to know what the future held for him. Even at this early stage, there were far too many uncertainties, and the situation could hardly be expected to improve if Juan decided to relocate.

On Saturdays the prospects for the rest of the day would be rather dull in Juan's home, the atmosphere awkward and tense after the pain and misery of Friday nights, while his parents hardly spoke to one another and preferred to stay indoors. Juan believe this was because they were deeply ashamed of their drunken behaviour and the hurtful things they said to one another.

Now the usual monotony of the Saturday lay ahead. The atmosphere that morning was no different from any other Saturday morning, and it was clear to him that his parents would be staying in bed for most of the day.

The most important thing for Juan on a Saturday morning was to deal with the after-effects of their Friday night. Trying to avoid his parents as far as possible, Juan would escape by going to the shops or visiting friends. Nothing exciting ever happened at home, and he constantly had to worry about the outcome of an argument between his parents. As usual, Juan went to visit one of his friends, a girl who was rather a special friend of his and spent most of the Saturday at her house.

"Last night was unusually quiet. All the time I was expecting something to happen, which is almost as bad as the real thing, as far as I am concerned". Juan told his friend.

"Juan, you'll see one day everything is going to change for the better. Don't give up now, keep focusing on the things you'd like to accomplish and keep a cool head." Juan's friend replied in a comforting tone of voice.

"I do try, but I just can't take it anymore. I'm sick and tired of struggling, tired of listening to the fighting, tired of making up excuses to cover up!"

She stroked his back while they were talking, hugged him, and he suddenly felt the prick of tears in his eyes. Acutely aware of the hopelessness of the situation in his home, he hugged her back. As the afternoon went by, he gradually felt more at peace, until suddenly realising how late it already was, he reluctantly had to make his way back home.

"Thanks for everything, and for allowing me to freely share my feelings with you," Juan told his friend.

"It's a pleasure, Juan, and remember you're always welcome in our home."

"Thank you so much! Love you always!"

"We love you too!" she replied.

"Well, I'll have to go now, enjoy the rest of the afternoon!"

"Thanks, Juan! You too and keep well!" waving as Juan walked out the gate.

As Juan walked in the front door, he heard his mother's voice coming from his parent's room, one moment sobbing and pleading with his father, and the next yelling at him, threatening to pack her things and leave.

"I don't know where I'll go. I'm jobless and penniless!" Elizabeth shouted. Juan immediately knew something is up.

These quarrels in the bedroom would typically go on around in vicious circles and ultimately come to nothing. Albert made no reply this time, it wouldn't have helped to try and understand why, as so many empty promises were made between them anyway, and life would just continue as before. Nothing has changed.

The rest of the day was spent in the usual aimless manner, while Juan tried to cheer them both up as best as he could. At supper time, Albert's place by the table in the window remained empty, while Elizabeth and Juan ate the usual meat, rice, and potatoes. Shortly after eight, the house was already in darkness and all three of us had gone to bed.

The atmosphere on Sundays could only be described as depressing, although, in a sense, Sunday had become a day of sobering up, and returning to a more normal routine. The one thing that did cheer them up, was Elizabeth's wonderful Sunday dinner.

Sunday dinner had, ever since Juan could remember, been somewhat of a tradition in their home, his mother doing all the preparation single-handedly. This was, in part, the reason why she didn't go to church as often as she would have liked. Another reason why she preferred to stay at home was that she felt uncomfortable with how she looked. The traces of the weekend's physical and emotional suffering were chiefly to blame for her shrinking away from attending church services, and her priorities had thus become to see Juan off to Sunday school instead, while Juan's father would sit in his wheelchair on the veranda, having a cigarette.

Although there was no school on Sundays, there was still Sunday school for Juan to attend. To him, it was far more stressful than an ordinary school day. With so many other kids attending Sunday school, it was a battle to make him to go. Juan had a critical sense of being watched by the others, being discussed and judged because of the clothes he was wearing. He also strongly suspected that people knew about the fighting and arguing in his home.

Following his mother's outburst of the previous day, the atmosphere was still strained. After, Albert had woken up and had summoned enough courage to emerge from his room, he was characteristically shy and withdrawn. Even the lovely food could not improve his mood on that Sunday, and shortly afterward Juan decided to go out and visit his friends and neighbours rather than staying at home the whole afternoon.

When he returned home late that afternoon, he saw that his mother was busy washing his father. Since he had lost his legs, it had become too inconvenient for him to wash. Washing him had turned out to be hell for both Juan's parents. Whereas previously Albert was free to do as he wished, he was now forced to rely on another to do this task for him.

On the one hand, Juan felt that his father had received his due punishment for the hell we had suffered: the nights alone outside in the cold, the fighting and the abuse, and the humiliation they had been put through.

Then again, Juan was moved by a deep pity for his father because of the terrible misfortune that had befallen him, for him it was like living on borrowed time. Everything he wanted or needed, had to be done for him by another person.

Although Juan did not know what had triggered the scene she had made the day before, he knew for certain that his mother had been endlessly patient with his father all through his ordeal thus far, washing him, bringing him his food, making his bed, and emptying the bottles he used to urinate in. It went beyond Juan's understanding every time his father had devastated her the way he did, even now that he was living a life in a wheelchair, he still found a way to hurt her.

So often had Juan wondered if it had become a habit for her, and sometimes even, if there was any pleasure to be gained from the situation.

Juan could hardly wait to write the final school exams. There was nothing he desired more than to move out of his parent's home and make a fresh start somewhere far from there, away from everything and everybody, away from the fighting, the arguing and the abuse. He was physically and emotionally drained. More than once he had considered committing suicide. Fortunately, he realised that suicide would not be the solution, but would only lead to further problems.

# Chapter 7.   Bloemfontein

As on any other morning, since Juan had started working in Bloemfontein, he was busy preparing for the humdrum of life in the city. It surprised him how easily he had slipped into this routine, to the point where he'd failed to notice the many beautiful things around him in the city that had become his new home.

'Why was I still alone at my age?' He thought, as he done his hair. He inspected himself in the mirror. Although it was true that there had been lovers, he was still living on his own. Deep inside of him, the memory of Jovi persisted, and this made him realise that being alone could never be a part of his personality.

Jovi was an extremely nice guy, and the two of them had understood one another well. More than once Juan had been at pains to explain to Jovi that living so far apart – the distance between Bloemfontein and Cape Town being more than a thousand kilometres – would be disastrous for a relationship between the two of them. This was so different from the kind of relationship where two people moved in with one another to be there for one another. Being in a relationship with another person on the other side of the world didn't seem a practical option for Juan.

Like most other people in Bloemfontein, Juan had to make use of a taxi to go to work, even if this was by no means the most agreeable means of transport for him. The city is much bigger than Beaufort West, getting around without a car of his own had proved to be a hassle. Sitting crammed into an overcrowded, noisy taxi, Juan was afforded very little chance of exploring his new surroundings.

Now and then, when the taxi stopped at a robot, he could catch a glimpse of one or two high buildings but found it impossible to identify specific places or landmarks of the city. That was one of the reasons why he preferred to get off the taxi some distance from his destination: by walking the rest of the way he found he could see and enjoy more of the city while getting familiar with the area where he worked at.

In the beginning, Juan doubted if he would ever be able to adapt himself to his new surroundings, but he had gradually become more clued-up and could later find his way around quite easily. It was a great relief to be away from home: now that he no longer had to listen to the fighting, he was far much more at peace. The difficult part of his life was being on his own, supporting himself was the greatest challenge of all.

Juan was working at the Waterfront, the biggest shopping mall he had ever seen, there were so many faces passing by, people and families hugging and greeting one another, babies crying, children laughing. There were escalators and lifts to accommodate the many people who flocked there to do their shopping at the mall, many shops and places of entertainment to choose from, including the restaurants, toy stores and cinemas that he loved to visit.

"Excuse me, sir, could you bring me a size-five shoe please," a client asked Juan.

"Certainly, madam. Please have a seat, while I find it for you quickly." Juan replied

"Thanks!"

In the storeroom at the back, the boxes were stacked haphazardly, and hunting for the correct shoe size could be frustrating. Knowing that the woman sat there waiting for him, he dashed around frantically and felt relieved when at last he found her size. As Juan hastened to the front, he removed the shoe from the box, and handed it to her.

Hurriedly she fitted the shoe on her foot. Availing himself of the necessary sales techniques, Juan took care to recommend the shoes to her.

"These look stunning on you, madam, but wait until you see them in red!" Juan tried to close the deal.

"Oh, thank you! Let's just have a look then, shall we?" the customer agreed.

Feeling confident that she would be buying this pair, he nevertheless went to fetch the red pair from the storeroom.

"I've just noticed that this is the last red pair, madam!" Juan informed the customer.

"You must be kidding me!" she replied.

"I've never been more serious! I can keep them aside for you for a little while if you prefer until you have decided which one you like best."

"Oh, that won't be necessary - I'll just take both pairs!" she answered.

Very happy and mightily pleased with himself, Juan went to the till to ring up the shoes.

"That will be two thousand four hundred, madam!"

"My goodness! You people aren't too cheap, are you?"

"Will it be cash for you?" Juan beamed, smiling at her.

"Yes, please!" she replied, taking out her purse and counting out the notes one by one.

"Can I have a slip please?" she requested.

"Of course, just a moment please!"

Rather meticulously, he put the two pairs of shoes in their boxes, reached down to take a white-and-silver carry bag out of the cupboard, to place the boxes into it.

"Enjoy your shoes! I hope to see you here again sometime!" Juan greeted her as she left.

"If God spares us, and our money lasts," she answered with a smile.

Before moving to Bloemfontein, Juan had wondered how easy or difficult it would be for someone new to relate to people here but soon realised that he had been unduly worried, as everybody here treated him with respect and greeted him with a smile.

During the day the shop had been very busy, and the time passed so quickly that before long it was already five o' clock. Juan was about to close the doors when a man came running towards him.

"Are you still open?" he asked.

"Yes, but we are about to closing," Juan replied.

"Could I quickly come in for a pair of shoes. I have a meeting tonight, and the ones I'm wearing now are broken."

"Please come inside!"

Juan let him in and locked the door behind them. At first, Juan felt trapped, trying his best to be reassured by the man's friendly smile. Juan had always been a gentle soul, too readily trusting of others, and often would be the first to get hurt.

"This shoe is perfect. I'll keep this one on if you will bring me the other one as well." he kindly requested.

"I'll do that."

Juan walked into the storeroom, feeling nervous, and kept looking back over his shoulder. There was nobody behind him, he told himself he was just overworked. He found the other shoe and took it to the front.

"Thanks a million! You're really saving my life. How much do I owe?" the man asked.

"It's nine hundred rands," Juan replied quickly. The man rummaged in his pocket, took out the money, and handed it over to him.

"One hundred, two hundred, three hundred, four hundred..." he counted until there was one thousand rand. Juan took the nine hundred and gave the man his extra one hundred back."

"No, no, no! You take it - as a little something for your trouble."

"No, sir, I can't do this!" Juan denied.

"Please take it, I insist!" the man insisted.

"Are you sure, sir?  A hundred rand is a lot of money!"

"I do know how to count, and I know the value of the money, but you've deserved it. Please keep it - go and buy yourself something with it," he said with a smile.

"Gosh, thank you, sir!" Juan stammered, putting the money in his pocket.

After the man had left, Juan quickly locked up. On my way out of the building, he met one of the security guards.

"Hello! I see you locked up on your own today?"

"Hi! Well, yes, the others are attending a course. I expect they will be back by tomorrow."

"I don't want to seem disrespectful, but may I ask you what your name is?" he asked.

"Juan."

"It's nice to meet you! My name is Ernesto." the guard replied.

"Nice to meet you, too!  So, what are you doing here?"

"Oh, I'm just checking to see that everything in the shops are in order."

"That's good. As long as you enjoy what you're doing." Juan said with a wondering eye.

"I do!  May I ask for how long you have been working here now?"

"Oh, not so very long. I'm from Beaufort West."

"That sounds familiar. I'm sure I passed through it on my way to Cape Town."

"Quite possibly! The road passing through it is one of only a few going to Cape Town." As soon as Juan had said that, they both burst out laughing.

Ernesto was a dark-skinned guy and almost as tall as Juan. Ernesto walked with Juan to the door, and Juan left feeling very happy indeed. It had turned out to be a wonderful day for him.

At home, later that evening, Juan reflected upon the encounter with Ernesto after work. He could not help feeling that there was more to it than meets the eye: there was just that something about Ernesto that did it for Juan. He immediately realised that he liked the guard. Still thinking about him, Juan filled the bath with water. As he stirred the water, he caught sight of his jiggly reflection in it. He first put one foot into the water, then the other, and tentatively lowered his body into the hot water.

Laying down on his back in the bath, Juan could hear his own heart beating. Never had he felt so at peace: no quarrels, no arguments, no verbal abuse. After he had finished bathing, he played a CD by Celine Dion, and as he became absorbed in the music, he found that he was again thinking of his meeting with Ernesto. Juan was looking forward to going to work the following day and was certain now that he had fallen in love with a stranger.

Juan was awake quite early, he put on his finest pair of trousers and a matching shirt. In the taxi, Juan was so absent-minded that he forgot to tell the driver where to let him off. Luckily the taxi stopped not too far from the Waterfront, and Juan was still within an easy walking distance from work. Like a child, excited to open a Christmas present, he could hardly wait to see Ernesto again and kept looking around while he was busy unlocking the door. Ernesto was nowhere to be seen.

"Good morning!" one of Juan's co-workers greeted him, Nicky.

"Hello! How are you this morning?" Juan replied.

"Very well thanks. The course was really worthwhile."

"I'm pleased to hear it, and it is great to know that you enjoyed it!"

Hurriedly, Juan went to fetch the bucket and mop and started cleaning the floor.

"So, were you busy yesterday?" Nicky asked.

"No, not really. It was a great day for me."

"What happened to you that you are so full of smiles today?" Nicky asked.

"Not much really! But I'm in love, and I feel as though I'm at last beginning to find my feet."

"In love?" he asked incredulously.

"Yes, you heard me, but more than that I can't tell you right now!" Juan replied, cutting the conversation short.

Despondently Juan looked at the wall clock later that day. It was half past three already, and he hadn't once caught sight of Ernesto. 'Had I been getting excited about nothing, hoping for something that was not even going to happen?' Juan thought, he then made up his mind to change the way he was thinking, and to focus his attention on the things that did matter instead. Later that afternoon, coming back from the toilets, Juan noticed someone standing in the corridor in front of the shop. From a distance, it looked like Ernesto, and as Juan came closer, he saw that it was indeed Ernesto standing there, Juan felt his heart was beating in his throat, and he could not stop himself from grinning ear to ear.

"Hello, how are you today?" Juan was the first to ask.

"Much better now that I've seen you!" Ernesto replied.

"Why is that?"

"Well, you are different from all the rest of the people here; it's really nice to see you!"

"What makes me stand out from the rest?" Juan asked with faked innocence.

"It's your personality," he replied.

"Well, that's good to hear! Are you going to stand here in front of our door all afternoon?"

"You can put it that way, yes!" Ernesto replied with a smile.

"Hmm...okay then, but I must go in now. See you later then?"

"We'll do that!" he said, sounding rather disappointed.

Juan tried to help each client as soon as they came into the shop but simply couldn't keep his eyes off Ernesto: he was the kind of man Juan had been dreaming of. Every now and then he passed by the shop, gazing at Juan with a smile on his face, and each time Juan acknowledged his presence with a wink and a smile.

Shortly before closing time, Juan had made up his mind to put his cards on the table. He grabbed a sheet of glossy paper from a shoebox, tore off a small scrap, and wrote on it what was on his mind. He knew it was far too soon to tell Ernesto how he felt, but Juan was in a flurry at that moment. As soon as everybody else had left, Juan quickly ran outside and handed Ernesto his note. He hastily unfolded and started to read it. Uncertain about what his reaction would be, Juan quickly locked up the shop and slipped out of the building unnoticed by him.

At home that night, Juan was still in a fluster and couldn't bring himself to settle down, all the time fervently hoping that he had done the right thing.

Juan's thoughts were interrupted when his cell phone suddenly started beeping. A text was coming through, and he was astonished to see that it came from Ernesto:

"Thanks for your note and your honesty. That is exactly how I feel!" the text read.

Juan read the message through four times. It felt so unreal. At first, he wanted to send him another message, or phone him back, but then decided against it. Perhaps it would be better to wait until the next day.

# Chapter 8.   A Year Later

The morning had started like any other. The fog covered the city, and Juan could hardly see the cars driving by as he stood gazing through the window.

He felt sad and despondent, convinced that there were negative things in the world just waiting for a time and place to happen. By now he had learned not to give up, and to keep moving on.

Juan decided to take it step by step, day by day. He realised now that he had been chasing a rainbow. So many troubles that he had to face, but he wouldn't let his spirit fail, not until he gets to his destination. Now that Ernesto and Juan were married, Juan had everything he ever dreamt of, yet the ghosts of his past hadn't disappeared. He was constantly reminded of the bad things, the things which tried to get to the better part of him.

Despite Ernesto's family's disapproval of their decision to get married, every day had proved to be a blessing for them. Juan had come to Bloemfontein to find himself, and to live a life of fulfilment, even though he had been hurt and pushed past the point of breaking.

On that very same day, Juan heard that his mother had also decided to undertake a journey to try and find her true self, choosing to leave Beaufort West and his father and to go and live with her brother in Welkom.

For Albert, the future had suddenly become utterly hopeless, a seemingly endless night without a sunrise. He was morbid and defeated, yet nobody could blame Elizabeth, who was totally exhausted by now. So many times, he had mistreated and humiliated her, and the time for her to move on had come.

Like Juan's mother, Juan found it difficult to open his heart to others, to talk about his secrets, hopes, and dreams, and to allow himself to show others his true self. As usual, he tried so hard to look stronger than he really was and therefore would hide his feelings all the time.

'Don't we all, at times, have to live through traumatic events, ultimately to come out stronger on the other side?' Thought Juan. And so, for many years, Juan had kept his feelings to himself. Being gay had been something he was hiding from others at all costs. He was afraid of what people would think of him, of how his parents would react, that his friends would push him away, and give up on him.

'Not all of us are afraid of who we are, or whether the world will accept us for whom we are,' Juan constantly thought. After he had met Ernesto, however, many things changed in his life, he was able to be his true self. Feeling more confident than ever before.

'People never tell you the way they truly feel, they are afraid of change, which is why they are miserable all the time,' Juan thought, 'I was still building walls around my heart. It was hard to forget. Because of the things that had happened to me, and the fear of that these bad things might just happen again,' Juan had started to distrust Ernesto.

Every text, call and working late excuse, seemed to pose a threat to their relationship. It is commonly acknowledged that one should trust one's instincts, and to let go when in doubt. For a long time, Juan had believed that love could heal all wounds, especially if one refrained from keeping a record of the wrongdoings of the other person.

It hurts to love someone, and not be loved in return, but what is more painful is to love someone that no longer cares for you. Sometimes in life we meet someone who means a lot you, only to find out, it was never meant to be, and that you just must let go of that person. Giving someone all your love is never an assurance that they will love you back, never expect love in return.

It was the third time that Ernesto had been cheating on Juan. Every time he had a valid excuse ready to safeguard himself, and Juan would readily forgive him. The last time, however, Juan had had enough, and could no longer handle the humiliation. Like his mother, Juan had decided to bring an end to this meaningless marriage.

Married life, as he knew it, opened his eyes to so many aspects of life, had also taught his heart to forgave. Juan was the dependable one in the relationship, who had always treated him with humility and honesty, and in the end, Juan was the one who got hurt. He was asking himself over and over' 'Why does it hurt so bad? Why do I feel so sad? even when I didn't love you.'

After Juan had seen him in the company of 'that girl', his heart seemed to stop for a few moments. Immediately Juan's future had become dark, and he felt utterly lost. He spent many hours blaming himself, looking for the fault within him, yet failing to understand why Ernesto would want to do this to him when he loved Ernesto so much, but leaving Ernesto was the best thing for Juan.


Early that morning Juan was busy cleaning the house when he heard a knock at the door. He quickly changed to something more suitable before hurrying down the passage to answer the door. The man who stood there was someone Juan had seen before, someone he saw one day as he was looking through his bedroom window one day.

"Hi! I'm sorry I took so long – I've been busy doing some cleaning. Please do come inside!"

"Not to worry, I'm used to everything." the man replied.

"Let's go through to the lounge." Juan offered.

While he followed Juan in, Juan wondered about the purpose of his visit.

"How can I help you?" Juan asked the man.

"I was wondering if I could use your parking for the next two days, if you won't be using it yourself, of course?"

"Yes certainly! There shouldn't be any problem. I don't own a car myself." Juan replied relieved.

"Thanks so much! I really appreciate it. Is there anything I can do to repay you?"

"Not at all! As I've said, I'm not using it now."

"I'm really grateful for this." the man replied with gratitude.

"Don't mention it. Can I offer you anything to drink?"

"No, thanks! I've got some work to do. Thanks once again!"

"It's a pleasure," Juan said, doing his best to be friendly while seeing the man out.

Having finished the housework, Juan felt exhausted and fell asleep on the couch in the lounge. Later that afternoon, he was awakened by a terrible commotion; for a while, Juan had forgotten about the neighbours who, by now, had become very jolly indeed. Looking through the window, he caught sight of all the empty bottles on the cemented area. With so many bottles standing around all over the place, the frenzy the party had reached by now wasn't at all surprising.

Juan thought to himself, 'How ironical that, even with so many people around us, life everywhere could be such a lonely experience.'

Dazzled by the setting sun's reflection in the big mirror on the wall, Juan closed the lounge curtains and went to my bedroom, where he opened one of the small side windows to let in some fresh air. For a long time, he just stood there breathing and relishing the sweet scents of the flowers.

He lay down on his bed, folding one of the small blue cushions between his arms. In his imagination, Juan relived the times Ernesto and he had been together, the happy times as well as the unhappy ones.

They have had so much to be thankful for. For a moment Juan pressed harder on the cushion and could imagine that Ernesto was still there. Even now that his place had become empty, and there was room for a new love, Juan's heart still refused to let go of him, knowing, too, that he hadn't deserved this heartache. With these thoughts still lingering in Juan's mind, he fell asleep.

Early the next morning, there was a loud knock on the door. Getting up slowly, still half asleep and without bothering to change, Juan sauntered to the front door. He looked through the tiny window to check who was there and saw the woman he had asked to come and do the cleaning.

"Good morning, Saria, how are you today?"

"Very well thank you! But I'm not so sure that the same can be said of you. Did you have a bad night?" she asked.

"No, actually I've slept quite well, although I must admit I've been having a spell of bad dreams lately, and I've also missed that someone I'm not supposed to be thinking of."

"Oh, don't I just know that feeling! It's almost two years now since my husband passed away, and most of the time I still have to force myself to go out of the house to face the world." she comforted me.

"That's exactly how I feel too. Come inside, let's make some coffee!"

Saria had been working for Juan for a couple of months, and already knew how to figure out his mood. Since they had been sharing many of their problems with one another, they had become quite familiar with each other's circumstances.

"Saria, being on my own last night, hasn't done me any good. With so much on my mind, especially missing him so much, I've slept rather badly. Will you make the coffee, please? Please make it strong!"

Juan went back to the bedroom and picked up his cell phone to check for messages. He wasn't sure who there might be a message from. Despite not having had contact with Ernesto for a long time, he was still expecting him to phone someday to make up for what had gone wrong between them. To say that he was sorry and wrong.

Saria came into the room with the coffee and sat down beside Juan on his bed.

"Everything will change for the better. I didn't believe this myself, but in the end, everything works out well," she said.

"I do hope you're right, sometimes there are just too many issues, and I feel as though I can't cope any further." Juan tried to explain.

"Can I run you your bath?" she interrupted him.

"Gosh, Saria! You really don't have to do this, but I wouldn't say no!"

Saria went and ran the bath, even adding bath foam to the water. Juan saw the foam clinging to the sides of her arms, he knew there was something therapeutic in their times together for her, that she stood there thinking about her husband as she dried her arms with one of the towels hanging on the wall.

"Your bath is ready, and you can just get in. I hope the water is warm enough. Don't wait too long!"

"I'm getting in straightaway, Saria! Thank you!"

For a long time, Juan laid in the bath, with a mug of coffee standing beside him on the edge of the bath. Juan drank the coffee slowly, in small mouthfuls, while enjoying the wonderful sensation of water on his skin: exactly what he had needed.

"Saria!" He called.

"Yes?"

"I just want to say thank you for everything you are doing for me. You always seem to know exactly what I need to make me feel better. Thank you so much for that!"

"It' s a pleasure. I appreciate your kind words."

Although it was still early in the day, the heat had already made itself felt, and Juan chose something light to wear. As he had to go for a haircut, he had to get ready to be on time for his appointment.

On his way to the hair salon, he stopped at the Waterfront to see if there would be any worthwhile movies showing in the afternoon. There was none that interest him, and he went on to a small restaurant for a quick bite.

At eleven o' clock he paid the bill and hurried to the salon. Juan was still on time yet sat there waiting patiently for ten minutes more before his turn came. He briefly told the hairdresser how he wanted his hair to be cut: short at the front, and longer at the back. Half an hour later he had finished with Juan's hair.

"It looks great! Thank you very much. How much do I owe?"

"Sixty-five rand," he replied.

I took four twenty-rand notes from my wallet and placed it on the counter.

"I'm feeling much better now. Please keep the change!"

"Thank you," the hairdresser replied. "Have a nice day!"

"You too!" Juan replied and left with a spring in his step.

On my way to say 'hello' to a friend, Juan saw a boy who stood begging at a robot. As Juan walked past him, the boy approached him for some money. For a moment the world stopped as Juan looked into his round, dark brown eyes, and read the pain and suffering there. Juan was about to say 'no' like all the other passers-by but then changed his mind. He closed his eyes, felt in his pocket, and counted the small change in his hand before taking some coins out and putting it in the boy's hands. Again, Juan looked into his eyes and got a strange feeling of déjà vu. Puzzled, he asked the boy some questions.

"Where do you live?"

"I am from this place but have no home," he replied.

"Why don't you have a home? Where are your parents?"

"They're still alive, but my father chased me away from home."

"Chased you away! Why would he do that?"

"He says I'm not his child, and that is why I'm standing here."

"He and my mother went on and on arguing and fighting about it, and that is how it came out," he replied with a tear running down his face.

"I am really terribly sorry to hear about this, but you must know that you can be helped. I will help you if you want to?"

"I'll be glad, but the small change will do for now!"

"It's a pleasure, but I do hope to see you again, and to help you in some other way, okay?"

"Okay, sir! Thanks a lot!"

"Just call me Juan. I have to run now, but I'll see you around then!"

"Go well."

As he walked away, not only did the whole incident seem incredibly strange to Juan, but there was also a bell ringing somewhere. The emotions were all too familiar, and he could have imagined what the boy must have been going through, especially being rejected by his father. A feeling Juan knew all too well.

The encounter caused old wounds to start bleeding. It was the kind of pain that never seemed to heal, and Juan would be reliving the heartache all over again. Sometimes we all have a lust for change, to change our situation and to forget about our pain and sorrows, but sometimes our situations is not our problems, but especially when the life around us gets into us, that is when our situation becomes our problems.

Juan soon realized that the past is the past. The best way to move forward was to wash off all the hurt and anger that he has collected along his journey, and to prepare himself for where he was going.

# Chapter 9.   Ronaldo

Some months later Juan was reading the newspaper at work when he noticed a report about a man who was due to appear in court after he had run over and killed his child. Having read the report, and inspected the photo more closely, Juan realised that the child was the boy he had spoken to on the street not so very long ago. Nausea came pushing up through his throat into his mouth. It was as though a lightning flash had pierced his heart.

Later that day Juan made several calls to find out when and where the funeral would be held.

He had decided to write a poem for the boy. As the time dragged on for the next two days, Juan saw the expression of the boy with the round brown eyes in the face of every child that he met. Those eyes had revealed the truth within his soul. His pain. His hopelessness.

Surprisingly, not many people turned out on the day of the funeral. How strange that such an exceptional boy should be buried in such a way. Juan was on the point of leaving the envelope containing the poem on the table among the few bunches of flowers that had been placed there when he decided instead to read it out loud after the minister had wrapped up his sermon.

"Like a wing on a bird, and heaven with a moon,

I thought we all belonged together.

With the thoughts of two people,

a storm broke loose over the blissful sea.

A tiny heart, steeped in oil

went on beating with difficulty.

With your eyes round and cold, as I remember them now,

it pierced my heart like a lightning flash.

I carried your heart with me,

and in this way could endure my own feelings.

I carry your heart within my own"

One could have heard a pin drop as Juan put the poem back in the envelope and placed it on the coffin. He felt the tears welling up in the corners of his eyes, and the pain cut straight through his heart. Juan thanked the minister, turned, and walked away.

For many months after the funeral, these events remained implanted in Juan's mind. Always having been an emotional kind of person, his heart could easily be moved by the suffering of another human being.

One evening at a club, close to the building where he worked at the time, Juan met the man of his dreams. A young man at the other end of the counter where Juan was sitting had captivated his attention. The man was well-dressed and attractive, with green eyes and short brown hair.

For an hour Juan just kept staring at him, until he could scrape together enough courage to start a conversation with the man.

"Hi! My name is Juan."

"Pleased to meet you! I'm Ronaldo."

Feeling rather awkward, and afraid of making a fool of himself, Juan answered, "I'm here on my own, and was wondering if I might join you for a chat?"

"By all means! I'm on my own too and could do with some company," he replied.

"Thank you! I must admit that for a moment I thought you might just think that I am being overboard being so forward!"

"If you did, I would have liked it," he laughed.

"Really? Seeing that we are speaking so plainly, I suppose I might as well admit that I have been watching you all the time."

"Well, to be quite honest, I was doing the same, and was hoping you would notice me."

"Amazing, isn't it?  Well, seeing as we are now sitting side by side, why don't we make the best of each other's company?"

And so, it happened that the two of them spent the evening chatting together. After a few drinks, they behaved as if they had known one another for a long time, gazing into one another's eyes like a newly married couple. Juan invited Ronaldo home with him, and they decided to start a relationship. Juan's heart rejoiced as he went to bed that night, still in that dreamy state of mind, and slept very soundly indeed.

Early the next morning, Juan could hardly wait to contact him. He hunted for his cell phone and, having found it, he immediately sent Ronaldo a message. Hours passed after that, and just as Juan's impatience started to get the better of him, Ronaldo phoned to ask what Juan was planning for the afternoon. Juan had no plans, and they immediately agreed upon a time and place to meet. Juan felt like a child on Christmas Eve. This was the relationship that he had been hoping for: it was almost too good to be true.

When the big silver clock on the wall said it was three o' clock, Juan brushed his teeth, checked himself in the mirror, and decided to go down to unlock the car. He felt so happy as he entered the lift, knowing that in just a few more minutes he would be seeing Ronaldo again. In the car, he played a CD by Whitney Houston and listened to it on his way to Ronaldo's place.

It was not far from where Juan lived, and some minutes later he stopped in front of Ronaldo's house, feeling deeply confident in himself and the future. Before Juan could phone to let Ronaldo know he was there, he had come outside to welcome Juan, and again he could barely believe all this was happening to him. For a while, they spent some time chatting away before Ronaldo suggested they go and visit a woman who was a good friend of his.

Juan wasn't very keen on this at first but later agreed. On their arrival at her place, he felt nervous.

"Where did you find this man, Ronaldo?" Kate questioned him.

"Oh, I just happened to be lucky enough to bump into him!"

"Hmm...where was that?" she asked again.

"Somewhere I never go," he answered hoping to change the subject.

"My goodness, you do know how to talk in circles, don't you?" she said.

Juan just stood there staring at the two of them, shaking his head.

The atmosphere in her home was very friendly, and Juan soon felt at ease. He had hardly sat down when she brought them each a glass of beer. As they were drinking their second glass, Kate's husband also arrived home.

Suddenly Juan was feeling uneasy all over again, but once it had become clear to him that the husband had no problem concerning their sexual orientation, Juan returned to his old self. While they were gathered there, so fully enjoying themselves, Juan took a picture of them and grew to like Ronaldo even more.

As the hours passed, the beer started to flow more and more freely. They talked about everything under the sun. Ronaldo and Juan also talked about their relationship, declaring their love for one another. Juan was on cloud nine, and he now firmly believed that this was the happiness he had been waiting for.

Later that night Juan chose one of the pictures he had taken of Ronaldo, as a background on his cell phone screen. With Ronaldo now occupying all Juan's thoughts, he fell asleep.

Early the next morning, Juan again sent Ronaldo a message. This time there was no response from him. Later that day Juan tried to phone him, and still no answer. In the back of his mind, the worst kind of suspicions was beginning to take shape. Juan consoled himself with the idea that Ronaldo might be busy working, and not allowed to carry his cell phone with him, or that he might not had had a chance to look at his messages.

Juan decided to compile a CD of all my favourite songs as a gift to him. This was usually the easiest way of conveying his feelings to other people. Music had always been an important part of his life, and he used it, whenever he could, to express his emotions. Again, Juan tried to send him a message, and after a while, there was still no response, Juan became worried about him, and over and over tried to contact him.

Juan got into a warm bath and decided to go out on his own. After having spent many hours at the club where he first met Ronaldo, and he still hadn't contacted Juan, he realised that Ronaldo was a love that lasted for one evening only. It now proved to be as he had feared – all too good to be true. Yet, there was still a tiny scrap of hope left in Juan, and he made the best of the rest of the night.

As the sun filtered through the curtain the next morning, his head felt like lead. Juan got up with a headache and went to the kitchen to help himself to painkillers. He was deeply hurt. Realising that once again he had been used, Juan couldn't take it anymore. He had dared to hope that this time it would be the real thing, and yet again he was left defeated.

He immediately typed Ronaldo a message to let him know exactly how he felt, and how much he had hurt Juan by giving Juan false hope. Juan laughed at himself when he saw in the mirror the tears that had come into his eyes, thinking 'How could I have been so stupid? How could I have trusted him so easily? Everybody walked over me, and still, I hadn't learned a lesson. How many more times did I yet have to suffer before I would learn life's lessons?'

Another day had come and gone. Still, Juan hadn't heard from Ronaldo. He seemed to have vanished into thin air, having taken a piece of Juan's heart along with him. A dark cloud was hanging over Juan, suffocating him. All the time he never stopped thinking of him.

The next morning, he woke up in the lounge after spending a miserable evening missing Ronaldo. Fingering the puffiness around his eyes, Juan looked for his cell phone where he had left it under a cushion, switched it on and waited, this time there was a message from Ronaldo. Excited and almost too scared to read it, Juan waited for a little while before opening it with trembling hands. Having toughened himself for the worst, he started to read it.

'I was terribly busy, so sorry I didn't send you a reply. Please forgive me. Love you!'

Juan did not believe a single word of that message, but his heart once again had betrayed his soul. He was still so madly in love with Ronaldo, that he would have believed him over and over, every time willing to forgive and start all over again. Later, feeling no desire to go anywhere, or to see anybody, Juan lay down on the couch listening to one of Adele's CDs.

He loved taking chances and going out. Juan was aware of all the suffering going on in the world around him, and in his own life too, but he would not allow it to get the better of him.

Although so many tears had been shed, and Juan had been through so much pain in his life, he could manage to remain cheerful, and to keep moving on. This time, however, it was different. He had difficulty shrugging off and coming to terms with the thoughts that haunted him and threatened to overpower him.

His heart was bleeding, and yet there were little bubbles prancing around in a breeze of hope. 'Where should I draw the line?' Juan thought, 'How could I tell my own heart that what I had believed in, was no longer valid, that hope had no right to exist? How could I make my heart listen to the voice of reason, not to give in to any feelings? Yes, my heart wanted him, I wanted to hold him, never to let him go. I wanted to hammer into his head and shout into his heart what I felt, and how much I cared for him.'

Ronaldo was so unlike Juan, where Juan was wild at heart, Ronaldo was calm and more composed. Juan would have sacrificed anything, was prepared to lose all he had, while Ronaldo would just sit around waiting. He consumed Juan's mind and filled every little nook of his being. Like a photo in a mirror, spun around to reflect myriad of images into Juan's being, Ronaldo penetrated each nerve of Juan's body.

The radio was on, and the presenters was talking, while Juan went on living in a world of his own, his mind dwelled on questions there were no answers to. Overwhelmed by all these painful thoughts, he called out to God and spoke with Him, the only one who ever really understood him and knew exactly what Juan went through. He didn't respond immediately yet talking with someone was the only thing Juan needed at the time.

There were so many things Juan didn't understand, thinking, 'Was I just stupid? Was I doing something wrong?' Juan prayed for himself, for inner strength, to be able to embrace and be at peace with himself. 'Was it okay to pray for me?' Juan continued thinking; 'Wouldn't it be better to pray for others, and for peace in the world? On the one hand, I felt thankful for still being alive, that I was so blessed to have both parents still alive, a roof over my head, transport, friends, and a job.' With these thoughts, Juan comforted himself and was able to receive the strength to carry on. 'One day at a time. Step by step.' He thought.

While all these thoughts weighed him down like a dark cloud hanging over, Juan switched off the radio and slipped a CD into the player. He heard the words of one of Adele's songs speaking to him, "To make you feel my love".

It stirred something deep within himself, and he followed the words in the booklet that came with the CD.

The song took him back to Ronaldo, but he had caused so much anger within Juan that he now would have preferred to hate Ronaldo. Juan wished that he had never met him. On the other hand, Juan was glad that meeting him, had changed so many things and had awakened within him an awareness of emotions he had never known before. Juan never knew that he could love someone so deeply as he had loved Ronaldo.

# Chapter 10. The Death of Juan's Mother

It was half-past two, the next morning when Juan received a call. Unwilling to answer and ignoring it at first. When the other telephone also started to ring, he had the uncanny feeling that someone was desperate to get a hold of him. Juan picked it up and heard someone on the other side talking in a soft voice.

"Juan, sorry to wake you up so early, but I have something to tell you, and the news that I am bringing is not good".

Juan just listened to the voice on the other side of the phone, without any reaction at first. It was when he heard the words,

"Your mother just passed away, she swallowed a handful of pills,"

when he dropped the phone. He sat up straight in bed, crossed his legs and arms. For almost an hour, he just sat upright, staring at the wall in front of him as tears ran down his face emotionless.

The moment felt so unreal as if he was in a nightmare. After a while, he came to his senses and realising what had happened, he washed his face, got dressed and headed for the Waterfront on his motorcycle.

Once there, he went to the second floor and found a quiet place to sit down, away from everything and everybody. His heart was broken, and his throat was aching as he gave himself over to floods of tears. After all, he had been through the last couple of days, his mother's death was the last thing on his mind. Now that she too had left him, his loneliness was even more acute.

Juan was angry, he was scared, he was lost somewhere between the heavens and earth. His life as he knew it, just ended. For so many years, she stood by his side. Even when she got punished. From birth she loved him. Every time she left, she did it for him, for them. He thought, 'Now she is gone, and what would become of me?'

Pulling himself together as best he could, he contacted the family by the phone number of the last missed call on my cell phone.

"Hello!"

"Hi, this is Juan speaking. I just wanted to know what happened, and where my mom is now."

"Your mother was upset about something, took various pills together in one go. She seemed okay, but after a while started trembling and vomiting. We then took her to hospital."

"And..."

"She was admitted, and they pumped her stomach, telling us she'd be fine, and that we would be able to take her home later in the evening. When we arrived there, the doctor told us he wanted her to stay in the hospital overnight. That is when she passed away."

"So she had taken her own life?"

"Well, yes. I am so sorry to have to tell you this, Juan. I wish it had been different."

It's okay. Thanks, I'll have to go now."

So many questions came rushing upon Juan. He shrank from what he had to do next but then took hold of the phone again.

"Hello, Dad!"

"Hello, how are you? Why do you phone so early in the morning?"

"It isn't all that early really. What are you busy with?" Juan asked his father.

"I'm just sitting in the kitchen. Why?"

"I have bad news to tell you, dad!"

"What's the matter?"

"Mom's not with us anymore," I answered, and started weeping.

"What are you talking about, Juan?"

"Dad, Mom died early this morning."

There was an outcry of anger and pain on the other side. Unable to restrain himself, Juan collapsed on the floor where he had been sitting. Never had he felt so much pain all at once. His life passed before his mind's eye in those moments. The one image that seemed to stand out from all the rest, was his mother's smile, almost like an advert on a page sticking out from a magazine.

'How could she just leave me, now that I still needed her more than ever? After all the misery, the fighting, Ernesto, the divorce, Ronaldo – now this?' Juan thought, 'She had been the one who had kept me going. She had given me life and had continued to love me unconditionally. Without ever expecting anything in return, and from the very bottom of her heart, she had given herself and every shred she had ever possessed.'

That day a big part of Juan died with her, thinking, 'What was I really feeling? Hate? Sadness? Had there ever been words to describe how it felt?' On the one hand, he felt relief to know that an end had come to her suffering, but deep inside of him he was, and still is, going through an endless amount of pain.

Selfishness makes people think only of themselves, their own loneliness and disorientation. She is no longer there to answer or explain why this had happened. At the time of her death his desire to live, all that he had achieved, and everything that went on in his life, had become insignificant. All his dreams had died with her.

Early the next week, everybody was notified of the cremation service. Juan had started to make plans to travel to Welkom, while his sister had also planned to travel from Hartenbos. The rest of the family likewise had plans in place to attend the service. Except for his father.

On the morning of the cremation, Juan's sister and he were lying in the bedroom where their mother had slept. Under no circumstances would they emerge from it before the time came to depart. They knew where they were going, and it felt as if Juan could lock himself in the room forever. Later they all got ready for the service and departed to the mortuary where the body was kept.

Juan got out of the car, and slowly approached the entrance to the building. The minister unlocked the door and invited them inside. In one of the corners of the hall, there was a small white cubicle with sliding doors where his mother's body was laying. At first, he couldn't bring himself to enter it, but the desire to see her again was stronger.

In a coffin under the glass cover, there she was - still, cold and serene. Her hair was tied back tightly, revealing the gold earrings her children had given her on Mother's Day. Her eyes were tightly closed and her mouth slightly puckered, so that it was impossible for him to even try to make himself believe she had a smile on her face. That was how he wanted to remember her, but it would have been a delusion. There were plenty of white candles and many different colours of roses arranged around the coffin. She, too, now looked like a rose to him.

Keeping his eyes on her face, Juan told himself that she was asleep. His heart was beating so fast, and he was crying. This was his mother – at this moment she was so near, yet so far. When the rest of the family had left the cubicle, Juan opened the lid and held her hand, telling her that he was no longer angry at her, and held nothing against her. Knowing that there was no longer any pain where she was now, was a consolation to him. He closed the lid, and still stood there gazing at her for a while longer. A part of him stayed there with her.

They had shared so much love and heartache, so many secrets, 'How was I to go on living meaningfully without her?' Juan thought again, 'What I had was what she had given me?"

"I'll miss you, I already do! Thank you for what you have done for me, for giving me my life, for the times you stood by me in every situation. I love you!"

Those were the last words Juan spoke to his mother.

Juan turned around and went to the car where the others were already waiting. They proceeded slowly behind the funeral carriage, heading for the church. He kept his eyes on the funeral carriage, all the time thinking about her being so near, yet lifeless. Having arrived at the church after a few minutes, his sister and he were reluctant to get out, they knew they would have to help carry the coffin into the church, both thinking, 'How could I do this knowing that it was her in that coffin?'

The coffin was standing on a beautiful silver trolley next to the funeral carriage and having braced themselves for what they had to do, they went towards it. Juan gripped the coffin's handle tightly, feeling her presence and her breath going through his body. The coffin was heavy, as though weighed down by the burden that she had to carry when she was still alive; likewise, there was a heaviness in Juan, like a thunderstorm before the rain came down. There was darkness too, and a coldness that seemed to match hers.

Juan's sister and he wept all through the service, each breath turning into a sob. It was unthinkable that they had to say their final farewell to the person they loved dearest, the one whom they had always looked up to, the person who comforted them in times of distress. The thought that they would never be able to see, hug or kiss her again, had them beside themselves with grief. To this day Juan still wishes that he could just hold her again in his arms.

After the service, they all returned to the house, where refreshments awaited family and friends who had come to the funeral. Juan had no need of anything to eat and headed for the room where he could be on his own. In those moments alone with himself, he accepted and made peace with what had happened.

The heavy mountain was still there weighing down on him those first few days after the funeral. Every step he took, was like wading through mud: it was an effort to get up every morning to face the day and to renew my appetite for life. Those first days were challenging for, getting used to the idea that his mother was no longer there was mind-blowing. Wherever Juan went there would be something or someone to remind him of her: women of her age with the same hair colour, mothers with kids walking past, or sitting in a restaurant, and it saddened him to see young people so lucky to still have their mothers with them.

Mothers are wonderful people. They understand everything, will be patient with you, and never give up hope. Juan thought often, wondering if people who are lucky enough to have their parents still alive, really appreciate them and realise what a blessing they truly are. If only they could understand that life is far shorter than we think.

Many people believe that suicide is an option and that no one has the right to take away that choice from you. Before we give up on life or making this horrible choice of suicide, give yourself a chance to get out of your own head.

Depression, anger, and misfortune are normal. We all must live with it. We can all take these negative things in life and see it as something positive. We need to reorder ourselves. Many of us, just like little Juan's mother had enough of life. She felt useless and no longer in control. She couldn't cope with the endless pain and abuse anymore.

She tried to pick up the pieces of her life for more than 40 years. She was exhausted and already lost. Even in the moment of absolute depression, we are still in control of our situation and life. All we need to do is to fight back. There is still so much to gain, so much greatness in pain. It makes us so much wiser and stronger.

# Chapter 11. Life Goes On

Sometime after the death of Elizabeth, Juan and a friend made the necessary arrangements to go and fetch his father in Beaufort West, not for a visit, but to come and live with him. Juan's father had always hoped that Elizabeth would one day return to him, but since her death had been left to face a void. Juan decided to fetch him so that they could at least console one another and share and cherish the memories they had of her.

When Juan and his friend arrived in Beaufort West one late afternoon, four years had passed since Juan had last been there. Walking through the house, it seemed smaller than he had remembered. His bed was still there in his old bedroom. Looking out through the window Juan noticed that the branches of the old apricot tree had been broken off. The grass seemed lifeless and the fence was sagging. Curious to see the backyard, he walked out and noticed that the old fig tree was still standing there. He remembered how he used to play under it in the old days, and he could still imagine his dog, Vlekkie, as she was laying under the tree in a patch of sunlight.

In the main bedroom, Juan noticed that only one side of the bed had been slept in. It was obvious that his father slept alone in his bed.

Most of the furniture in the house had already been sold, and the rest they no longer needed anymore. Everything was ready and packed up, but since they had decided to stay over for the night, and to depart early the next morning, Juan now had the opportunity to go for a walk through the town.

In the main street, Juan sat down for a while on the bench in front of the church, a cool breeze touching his shoulders. In the deepening twilight, he relived some of his childhood adventures, as clearly as if it had been only yesterday that everything had happened to him.

When the church clock struck seven o clock, he decided to go and say 'hello' to a girl who had been a long-time friend. He walked to the house where she and her family were living and knocked at the familiar grey door. Juan could hear approaching footsteps in the passage, and then the door was opened.

"Hi, Ans! My goodness, you look great!"

Tears came into her eyes, and she hugged Juan tightly.

"This is such a great surprise! Where are you living nowadays?" she asked me.

"I'm still in Bloemfontein, and I've come to fetch my father to live with me there," Juan replied.

"I am so sorry about your mother! It came as a great shock to me." She said, empathising with him.

"I'm okay now. I've had time to make peace with the fact that she is no longer there." Juan replied.

"Please come in! I'll make us some coffee. Let's go through to the kitchen."

Juan followed her to the kitchen, and it was almost like being two school kids again. While they were drinking coffee in the kitchen, Juan had the chance to tell her everything that had happened to him. Like in the good old days, they could open their hearts to one another, and feel lighter after having shared our deepest feelings with one another. It was nearly two hours later before Juan went back home.

Sleeping next to his father on his bed that night, was touching to notice that he seemed so happy to have Juan there, he slept like a baby. We got up early the next morning, and after eating the breakfast Juan had prepared for the three of them, got rid of the last few things, packed what was left, and loaded the car.

At half past ten, they stopped at the filling-station before starting off on their journey to Bloemfontein. Albert was very excited, and so was Juan. They never stopped talking about Bloemfontein, what it was like, and what they would do once they were settled in. Juan, his friend and his father arrived in Bloemfontein in the late afternoon. Once they had finished unpacking, they went to a nearby restaurant for something to eat.

A few months later Juan's father relapsed into his old drinking habits. Arriving home one afternoon after work, Juan saw him stone drunk in the lounge. Juan greeted him and went to the kitchen. Unnoticed by him, Juan managed to go to his room where he found what he already suspected – an almost empty bottle of brandy. Juan was furious yet managed to stay outwardly calm.  In the lounge, they exchanged a few words.

After a few more minutes and another drink, Albert started talking about Juan's mother, blaming and slandering her.  As he went on about the real reason why she had left him at the time, how she had been tired of him, and he had meant nothing to her sexually, because he was in a wheelchair, Juan managed to remain silent.

It did not stop there, one moment he would be dwelling on the past, blaming Juan for his mother's death because he was gay, and the next he would be telling Juan that he wasn't his child. To Juan, it seemed that by throwing around all these accusations, he was showing his true colours that night. As they started quarrelling, and so many things were uttered that should have remained unsaid, Juan plucked him out of his wheelchair. The world had suddenly come to a standstill. They both remained silent then. After Juan had picked him up again, he immediately went to his room, slamming the door behind him.

For almost two days, he locked himself up in his room. Juan decided to leave him alone to allow him to come to his senses again, while Juan begged God to forgive him for lifting his hands against his father. He just wished to be able to look him in the eye again.

Nothing was said between the two of them for some days to come. Then one morning he came to Juan and asked Juan to forgive him. It was the first time ever since Juan could remember, that he heard his father say he was sorry for anything he had done in a tone of true remorse. Juan was speechless and embraced his father close to his chest, telling him that he was no longer angry. Juan forgave him, even though what he had said had cut deeply and painfully into Juan's being. Only because Juan loved his father, could he try to bury the hurt caused by the harshness of those bitter words. What Juan did was even worse, laying a hand on his own father. This is also unforgiving.

Nowadays, as Juan drove or walked through the streets of Bloemfontein, or sit behind his desk at work, the memory of his mother still haunts him. He feels lonely and long for someone with whom he can share his life – somebody who will understand him and love him unconditionally. Having lost so much and having passed through so much pain in his life, he needs someone he can lean on to.

'Life is hard, but can also be beautiful, depending on what we make of it.' Juan thought, 'I have learned to accept it, and to make it agreeable for myself by always being honest and sincere. What has happened in the past has made me stronger as a person, has taught me what is right, and how to treat and appreciate others. What they say about living in houses of glass has begun to make a lot of sense to me. To be careful what you say, not to make promises that you cannot keep, and not to talk of love and take someone's heart into your hands if you know fully well that you are unable to love in return: these are the rules that I have come to live by.'

Three years after the suicide of Juan's mother, his father passed away. He was terribly sick and spent his last days in a local hospital. Juan and his father had three years to bond and in that three years found each other again.

Juan never thought that he could feel happy and complete again, he found a way to pick up the pieces, and reorder his life. He never even thought that he would live to see his 30's. Juan is not only a survivor of domestic abuse and relentless pain and misfortune, but he has gained so much in life.

Juan had met someone that means the world to him. Someone he can trust. For the very first time, he doesn't have to look over his shoulder anymore. He is living his dream life. Making the best of every moment and any situation he finds himself in. He has learned that we should be bold enough to use our voices, to be brave enough to listen to our hearts and to be strong enough to live the life we have imagined.

------------

Only you can decide when you need to change the direction of your life. In those moments of frustration and doubt, and when you have worked so hard for success but only see evidence to the contrary, take a break to reorder your life and your thinking. Maybe redefine your goals. Don't keep your past alive by watching it, thinking about it all the time, talking about it repeatedly. We must let our past go. We must forgive people who have hurt us, if we don't, those people keep the power over us, and through this we poison ourselves.

Throughout Juan's life, he has experienced hurt, pain, resentment, psychological abuse and he was alone. He went through an emotional rollercoaster of falling in love, marriage, divorce and emotional abuse. Juan lost his mother due to suicide and soon thereafter lost his father due to illness. Despite so many pain and suffering, Juan still found a way to be strong. Juan kept on believing in himself. He made peace with everything, he learnt to forgave and to move on. Suicide was never an option. It was all about forgiveness and to let go off his past. Be free. Stop locking yourself up in the prison of your past.